The Tale of a Tub and The History of Martin

The Tale of a Tub and The History of Martin

Jonathan Swift

MINT EDITIONS

The Tale of a Tub and The History of Martin was first published in 1704.

This edition published by Mint Editions 2020.

ISBN 9781513270272 | E-ISBN 9781513275277

Published by Mint Editions®

 MINT EDITIONS

minteditionbooks.com

Publishing Director: Jennifer Newens
Design & Production: Rachel Lopez Metzger
Project Manager: Micaela Clark
Typesetting: Westchester Publishing Services

Contents

THE HISTORY OF MARTIN

A TALE OF A TUB

My Lord,

Though the author has written a large Dedication, yet that being addressed to a Prince whom I am never likely to have the honour of being known to; a person, besides, as far as I can observe, not at all regarded or thought on by any of our present writers; and I being wholly free from that slavery which booksellers usually lie under to the caprices of authors, I think it a wise piece of presumption to inscribe these papers to your Lordship, and to implore your Lordship's protection of them. God and your Lordship know their faults and their merits; for as to my own particular, I am altogether a stranger to the matter; and though everybody else should be equally ignorant, I do not fear the sale of the book at all the worse upon that score. Your Lordship's name on the front in capital letters will at any time get off one edition: neither would I desire any other help to grow an alderman than a patent for the sole privilege of dedicating to your Lordship.

I should now, in right of a dedicator, give your Lordship a list of your own virtues, and at the same time be very unwilling to offend your modesty; but chiefly I should celebrate your liberality towards men of great parts and small fortunes, and give you broad hints that I mean myself. And I was just going on in the usual method to peruse a hundred or two of dedications, and transcribe an abstract to be applied to your Lordship, but I was diverted by a certain accident. For upon the covers of these papers I casually observed written in large letters the two following words, DETUR DIGNISSIMO, which, for aught I knew, might contain some important meaning. But it unluckily fell out that none of the Authors I employ understood Latin (though I have them often in pay to translate out of that language). I was therefore compelled to have recourse to the Curate of our Parish, who Englished it thus, *Let it be given to the worthiest*; and his comment was that the Author meant his work should be dedicated to the sublimest genius of the age for wit, learning, judgment, eloquence, and wisdom. I called at a poet's chamber (who works for my shop) in an alley hard by, showed him the translation, and desired his opinion who it was that the Author could mean. He told me, after some consideration, that vanity was a thing he abhorred, but by the description he thought himself to be the person aimed at; and at the same time he very kindly offered his own assistance gratis towards penning a dedication to himself. I desired him, however, to give a second guess. Why then, said he, it must be I, or my Lord Somers. From thence I went to several other wits of my acquaintance, with no small hazard and weariness to my person, from a prodigious number of dark winding stairs; but found them all in the same story, both of your Lordship and themselves. Now your Lordship is to understand that this proceeding was not of my own invention; for I have somewhere heard it is a maxim that those to whom everybody allows the second place have an undoubted title to the first.

This infallibly convinced me that your Lordship was the person intended by the Author. But being very unacquainted in the style and form of dedications, I employed those wits aforesaid to furnish me with hints and materials towards a panegyric upon your Lordship's virtues.

In two days they brought me ten sheets of paper filled up on every side. They swore to me that they had ransacked whatever could be found in the characters of Socrates, Aristides, Epaminondas, Cato, Tully, Atticus, and other hard names which I cannot now recollect. However, I have reason to believe they imposed upon my ignorance, because when I came to read over their collections, there was not a syllable there but what I and everybody else knew as well as themselves: therefore I grievously suspect a cheat; and that these Authors of mine stole and transcribed every word from the universal report of mankind. So that I took upon myself as fifty shillings out of pocket to no manner of purpose.

If by altering the title I could make the same materials serve for another dedication (as my betters have done), it would help to make up my loss; but I have made several persons dip here and there in those papers, and before they read three lines they have all assured me plainly that they cannot possibly be applied to any person besides your Lordship.

I expected, indeed, to have heard of your Lordship's bravery at the head of an army; of your undaunted courage in mounting a breach or scaling a wall; or to have had your pedigree traced in a lineal descent from the House of Austria; or of your wonderful talent at dress and dancing; or your profound knowledge in algebra, metaphysics, and the Oriental tongues: but to ply the world with an old beaten story of your wit, and eloquence, and learning, and wisdom, and justice, and politeness, and candour, and evenness of temper in all scenes of life; of that great discernment in discovering and readiness in favouring deserving men; with forty other common topics; I confess I have neither conscience nor countenance to do it. Because there is no virtue either of a public or private life which some circumstances of your own have not often produced upon the stage of the world; and those few which for want of occasions to exert them might otherwise have passed unseen or unobserved by your friends, your enemies have at length brought to light.

It is true I should be very loth the bright example of your Lordship's virtues should be lost to after-ages, both for their sake and your own; but chiefly because they will be so very necessary to adorn the history of a late reign; and that is another reason why I would forbear to make a recital of them here; because I have been told by wise men that as dedications have run for some years past, a good historian will not be apt to have recourse thither in search of characters.

There is one point wherein I think we dedicators would do well to change our measures; I mean, instead of running on so far upon the praise of our patron's liberality, to spend a word or two in admiring their patience. I can put no greater compliment on your Lordship's than by giving you so ample an occasion to exercise it at present. Though perhaps I shall not be apt to reckon much merit to your Lordship upon that score, who having been formerly used to tedious harangues, and sometimes to as little purpose, will be the readier to pardon this, especially when it is offered by one who is, with all respect and veneration,

My Lord,
        Your Lordship's most obedient
            and most faithful Servant,
                THE BOOKSELLER

The Bookseller to the Reader

I t is now six years since these papers came first to my hand, which seems to have been about a twelvemonth after they were written, for the Author tells us in his preface to the first treatise that he had calculated it for the year 1697; and in several passages of that discourse, as well as the second, it appears they were written about that time.

As to the Author, I can give no manner of satisfaction. However, I am credibly informed that this publication is without his knowledge, for he concludes the copy is lost, having lent it to a person since dead, and being never in possession of it after; so that, whether the work received his last hand, or whether he intended to fill up the defective places, is like to remain a secret.

If I should go about to tell the reader by what accident I became master of these papers, it would, in this unbelieving age, pass for little more than the cant or jargon of the trade. I therefore gladly spare both him and myself so unnecessary a trouble. There yet remains a difficult question—why I published them no sooner? I forbore upon two accounts. First, because I thought I had better work upon my hands; and secondly, because I was not without some hope of hearing from the Author and receiving his directions. But I have been lately alarmed with intelligence of a surreptitious copy which a certain great wit had new polished and refined, or, as our present writers express themselves, "fitted to the humour of the age," as they have already done with great felicity to Don Quixote, Boccalini, La Bruyère, and other authors. However, I thought it fairer dealing to offer the whole work in its naturals. If any gentleman will please to furnish me with a key, in order to explain the more difficult parts, I shall very gratefully acknowledge the favour, and print it by itself.

The Epistle Dedicatory to his Royal Highness Prince Posterity

Sir,

I here present your Highness with the fruits of a very few leisure hours, stolen from the short intervals of a world of business, and of an employment quite alien from such amusements as this; the poor production of that refuse of time which has lain heavy upon my hands during a long prorogation of Parliament, a great dearth of foreign news, and a tedious fit of rainy weather. For which, and other reasons, it cannot choose extremely to deserve such a patronage as that of your Highness, whose numberless virtues in so few years, make the world look upon you as the future example to all princes. For although your Highness is hardly got clear of infancy, yet has the universal learned world already resolved upon appealing to your future dictates with the lowest and most resigned submission, fate having decreed you sole arbiter of the productions of human wit in this polite and most accomplished age. Methinks the number of appellants were enough to shock and startle any judge of a genius less unlimited than yours; but in order to prevent such glorious trials, the person, it seems, to whose care the education of your Highness is committed, has resolved, as I am told, to keep you in almost an universal ignorance of our studies, which it is your inherent birthright to inspect.

It is amazing to me that this person should have assurance, in the face of the sun, to go about persuading your Highness that our age is almost wholly illiterate and has hardly produced one writer upon any subject. I know very well that when your Highness shall come to riper years, and have gone through the learning of antiquity, you will be too curious to neglect inquiring into the authors of the very age before you; and to think that this insolent, in the account he is preparing for your view, designs to reduce them to a number so insignificant as I am ashamed to mention; it moves my zeal and my spleen for the honour and interest of our vast flourishing body, as well as of myself, for whom I know by long experience he has professed, and still continues, a peculiar malice.

It is not unlikely that, when your Highness will one day peruse what I am now writing, you may be ready to expostulate with your governor upon the credit of what I here affirm, and command him to show you some of our productions. To which he will answer—for I am well informed of his designs—by asking your Highness where they are, and what is become of them? and pretend it a demonstration that there never were any, because they are not then to be found. Not to be found! Who has mislaid them? Are they sunk in the abyss of things? It is certain that in their own nature they were light enough to swim upon the surface for all eternity; therefore, the fault is in him who tied weights so heavy to their heels as to depress them to the centre. Is their very essence destroyed? Who has annihilated them? Were they drowned by purges or martyred by pipes? Who administered them to the posteriors of —. But that it may no longer be a doubt with your Highness who is to be the author of this universal ruin, I beseech you to observe that large and terrible scythe which your governor affects to bear continually about him. Be pleased to remark the length and strength, the sharpness and hardness, of his nails and teeth; consider his baneful, abominable breath, enemy to life and matter, infectious and corrupting, and then reflect whether it be possible for any mortal ink and paper of this generation to make a suitable resistance. Oh, that your Highness would one day resolve to disarm this usurping *maître de palais* of his furious engines, and bring your empire *hors du page*.

It were endless to recount the several methods of tyranny and destruction which your governor is pleased to practise upon this occasion. His inveterate malice is such to the writings of our age, that, of several thousands produced yearly from this renowned city, before the next revolution of the sun there is not one to be heard of. Unhappy infants! many of them barbarously destroyed before they have so much as learnt their mother-tongue to beg for pity. Some he stifles in their cradles, others he frights into convulsions, whereof they suddenly die, some he flays alive, others he tears limb from limb, great numbers are offered to Moloch, and the rest, tainted by his breath, die of a languishing consumption.

But the concern I have most at heart is for our Corporation of Poets, from whom I am preparing a petition to your Highness, to be subscribed with the names of one hundred and thirty-six of the first race, but whose immortal productions are never likely to reach your eyes, though each of them is now an humble and an earnest appellant for the laurel, and has large comely volumes ready to show for a support to his pretensions. The never-dying works of these illustrious persons your governor, sir, has devoted to unavoidable death, and your Highness is to be made believe that our age has never arrived at the honour to produce one single poet.

We confess immortality to be a great and powerful goddess, but in vain we offer up to her our devotions and our sacrifices if your Highness's governor, who has usurped the priesthood, must, by an unparalleled ambition and avarice, wholly intercept and devour them.

To affirm that our age is altogether unlearned and devoid of writers in any kind, seems to be an assertion so bold and so false, that I have been sometimes thinking the contrary may almost be proved by uncontrollable demonstration. It is true, indeed, that although their numbers be vast and their productions numerous in proportion, yet are they hurried so hastily off the scene that they escape our memory and delude our sight. When I first thought of this address, I had prepared a copious list of titles to present your Highness as an undisputed argument for what I affirm. The originals were posted fresh upon all gates and corners of streets; but returning in a very few hours to take a review, they were all torn down and fresh ones in their places. I inquired after them among readers and booksellers, but I inquired in vain; the memorial of them was lost among men, their place was no more to be found; and I was laughed to scorn for a clown and a pedant, devoid of all taste and refinement, little versed in the course of present affairs, and that knew nothing of what had passed in the best companies of court and town. So that I can only avow in general to your Highness that we do abound in learning and wit, but to fix upon particulars is a task too slippery for my slender abilities. If I should venture, in a windy day, to affirm to your Highness that there is a large cloud near the horizon in the form of a bear, another in the zenith with the head of an ass, a third to the westward with claws like a dragon; and your Highness should in a few minutes think fit to examine the truth, it is certain they would be all chanced in figure and position, new ones would arise, and all we could agree upon would be, that clouds there were, but that I was grossly mistaken in the zoography and topography of them.

But your governor, perhaps, may still insist, and put the question, What is then become of those immense bales of paper which must needs have been employed in such numbers of books? Can these also be wholly annihilated, and to of a sudden, as I pretend? What shall I say in return of so invidious an objection? It ill befits the distance between your Highness and me to send you for ocular conviction to a jakes or an oven, to the windows of a bawdyhouse, or to a sordid lanthorn. Books, like men their authors, have no more than one way of coming into the world, but there are ten thousand to go out of it and return no more.

I profess to your Highness, in the integrity of my heart, that what I am going to say is literally true this minute I am writing; what revolutions may happen before it shall be ready for your perusal I can by no means warrant; however, I beg you to accept it as a specimen of our learning, our politeness, and our wit. I do therefore affirm, upon the word of a sincere man, that there is now actually in being a certain poet called John Dryden, whose translation of Virgil was lately printed in large folio, well bound, and if diligent search were made, for aught I know, is yet to be seen. There is another called Nahum Tate, who is ready to make oath that he has caused many reams of verse to be published, whereof both himself and his bookseller, if lawfully required, can still produce authentic copies, and therefore wonders why the world is pleased to make such a secret of it. There is a third, known by the name of Tom Durfey, a poet of a vast comprehension, an universal genius, and most profound learning. There are also one Mr. Rymer and one Mr. Dennis, most profound critics. There is a person styled Dr. Bentley, who has wrote near a thousand pages of immense erudition, giving a full and true account of a certain squabble of wonderful importance between himself and a bookseller; he is a writer of infinite wit and humour, no man rallies with a better grace and in more sprightly turns. Further, I avow to your Highness that with these eyes I have beheld the person of William Wotton, B.D., who has written a good-sized volume against a friend of your governor, from whom, alas! he must therefore look for little favour, in a most gentlemanly style, adorned with utmost politeness and civility, replete with discoveries equally valuable for their novelty and use, and embellished with traits of wit so poignant and so apposite, that he is a worthy yoke-mate to his fore-mentioned friend.

Why should I go upon farther particulars, which might fill a volume with the just eulogies of my contemporary brethren? I shall bequeath this piece of justice to a larger work, wherein I intend to write a character of the present set of wits in our nation; their persons I shall describe particularly and at length, their genius and understandings in miniature.

In the meantime, I do here make bold to present your Highness with a faithful abstract drawn from the universal body of all arts and sciences, intended wholly for your service and instruction. Nor do I doubt in the least but your Highness will peruse it as carefully and make as considerable improvements as other young princes have already done by the many volumes of late years written for a help to their studies.

That your Highness may advance in wisdom and virtue, as well as years, and at last outshine all your royal ancestors, shall be the daily prayer of,

SIR,

Your Highness's most devoted, &c.

Decemb. 1697

The Preface

The wits of the present age being so very numerous and penetrating, it seems the grandees of Church and State begin to fall under horrible apprehensions lest these gentlemen, during the intervals of a long peace, should find leisure to pick holes in the weak sides of religion and government. To prevent which, there has been much thought employed of late upon certain projects for taking off the force and edge of those formidable inquirers from canvassing and reasoning upon such delicate points. They have at length fixed upon one, which will require some time as well as cost to perfect. Meanwhile, the danger hourly increasing, by new levies of wits, all appointed (as there is reason to fear) with pen, ink, and paper, which may at an hour's warning be drawn out into pamphlets and other offensive weapons ready for immediate execution, it was judged of absolute necessity that some present expedient be thought on till the main design can be brought to maturity. To this end, at a grand committee, some days ago, this important discovery was made by a certain curious and refined observer, that seamen have a custom when they meet a Whale to fling him out an empty Tub, by way of amusement, to divert him from laying violent hands upon the Ship. This parable was immediately mythologised; the Whale was interpreted to be Hobbes's "Leviathan," which tosses and plays with all other schemes of religion and government, whereof a great many are hollow, and dry, and empty, and noisy, and wooden, and given to rotation. This is the Leviathan from whence the terrible wits of our age are said to borrow their weapons. The Ship in danger is easily understood to be its old antitype the commonwealth. But how to analyse the Tub was a matter of difficulty, when, after long inquiry and debate, the literal meaning was preserved, and it was decreed that, in order to prevent these Leviathans from tossing and sporting with the commonwealth, which of itself is too apt to fluctuate, they should be diverted from that game by "A Tale of a Tub." And my genius being conceived to lie not unhappily that way, I had the honour done me to be engaged in the performance.

This is the sole design in publishing the following treatise, which I hope will serve for an interim of some months to employ those unquiet spirits till the perfecting of that great work, into the secret of which it is reasonable the courteous reader should have some little light.

It is intended that a large Academy be erected, capable of containing nine thousand seven hundred forty and three persons, which, by modest computation, is reckoned to be pretty near the current number of wits in this island. These are to be disposed into the several schools of this Academy, and there pursue those studies to which their genius most inclines them. The undertaker himself will publish his proposals with all convenient speed, to which I shall refer the curious reader for a more particular account, mentioning at present only a few of the principal schools. There is, first, a large pederastic school, with French and Italian masters; there is also the spelling school, a very spacious building; the school of looking-glasses; the school of swearing; the school of critics; the school of salivation; the school of hobby-horses; the school of poetry; the school of tops; the school of spleen; the school of gaming; with many others too tedious to recount. No person to be admitted member into any of these schools without an attestation under two sufficient persons' hands certifying him to be a wit.

But to return. I am sufficiently instructed in the principal duty of a preface if my genius, were capable of arriving at it. Thrice have I forced my imagination to take the tour of my invention, and thrice it has returned empty, the latter having been wholly drained by the following treatise. Not so my more successful brethren the moderns, who will by no means let slip a preface or dedication without some notable distinguishing stroke to surprise the reader at the entry, and kindle a wonderful expectation of what is to ensue. Such was that of a most ingenious poet, who, soliciting his brain for something new, compared himself to the hangman and his patron to the patient. This was *insigne, recens, indictum ore alio*. When I went through that necessary and noble course of study, I had the happiness to observe many such egregious touches, which I shall not injure the authors by transplanting, because I have remarked that nothing is so very tender as a modern piece of wit, and which is apt to suffer so much in the carriage. Some things are extremely witty to-day, or fasting, or in this place, or at eight o'clock, or over a bottle, or spoke by Mr. Whatdyecall'm, or in a summer's morning, any of which, by the smallest transposal or misapplication, is utterly annihilate. Thus wit has its walks and purlieus, out of which it may not stray the breadth of a hair, upon peril of being lost. The moderns have artfully fixed this Mercury, and reduced it to the circumstances of time, place, and person. Such a jest there is that will not pass out of Covent Garden, and such a one that is nowhere intelligible but at Hyde Park Corner. Now, though it sometimes tenderly affects me to consider that all the towardly passages I shall deliver in the following treatise will grow quite out of date and relish with the first shifting of the present scene, yet I must need subscribe to the justice of this proceeding, because I cannot imagine why we should be at expense to furnish wit for succeeding ages, when the former have made no sort of provision for ours; wherein I speak the sentiment of the very newest, and consequently the most orthodox refiners, as well as my own. However, being extremely solicitous that every accomplished person who has got into the taste of wit calculated for this present month of August 1697 should descend to the very bottom of all the sublime throughout this treatise, I hold it fit to lay down this general maxim. Whatever reader desires to have a thorough comprehension of an author's thoughts, cannot take a better method than by putting himself into the circumstances and posture of life that the writer was in upon every important passage as it flowed from his pen, for this will introduce a parity and strict correspondence of ideas between the reader and the author. Now, to assist the diligent reader in so delicate an affair— as far as brevity will permit—I have recollected that the shrewdest pieces of this treatise were conceived in bed in a garret. At other times (for a reason best known to myself) I thought fit to sharpen my invention with hunger, and in general the whole work was begun, continued, and ended under a long course of physic and a great want of money. Now, I do affirm it will be absolutely impossible for the candid peruser to go along with me in a great many bright passages, unless upon the several difficulties emergent he will please to capacitate and prepare himself by these directions. And this I lay down as my principal *postulatum*.

Because I have professed to be a most devoted servant of all modern forms, I apprehend some curious wit may object against me for proceeding thus far in a preface without declaiming, according to custom, against the multitude of writers whereof the whole multitude of writers most reasonably complain. I am just come from perusing some hundreds of prefaces, wherein the authors do at the very beginning address the gentle reader concerning this enormous grievance. Of these I have preserved a few examples, and shall set them down as near as my memory has been able to retain them.

One begins thus: "For a man to set up for a writer when the press swarms with," &c.

Another: "The tax upon paper does not lessen the number of scribblers who daily pester," &c.

Another: "When every little would-be wit takes pen in hand, 'tis in vain to enter the lists," &c.

Another: "To observe what trash the press swarms with," &c.

Another: "Sir, it is merely in obedience to your commands that I venture into the public, for who upon a less consideration would be of a party with such a rabble of scribblers," &c.

Now, I have two words in my own defence against this objection. First, I am far from granting the number of writers a nuisance to our nation, having strenuously maintained the contrary in several parts of the following discourse; secondly, I do not well understand the justice of this proceeding, because I observe many of these polite prefaces to be not only from the same hand, but from those who are most voluminous in their several productions; upon which I shall tell the reader a short tale.

A mountebank in Leicester Fields had drawn a huge assembly about him. Among the rest, a fat unwieldy fellow, half stifled in the press, would be every fit crying out, "Lord! what a filthy crowd is here. Pray, good people, give way a little. Bless need what a devil has raked this rabble together. Z—ds, what squeezing is this? Honest friend, remove your elbow." At last a weaver that stood next him could hold no longer. "A plague confound you," said he, "for an overgrown sloven; and who in the devil's name, I wonder, helps to make up the crowd half so much as yourself? Don't you consider that you take up more room with that carcass than any five here? Is not the place as free for us as for you? Bring your own guts to a reasonable compass, and then I'll engage we shall have room enough for us all."

There are certain common privileges of a writer, the benefit whereof I hope there will be no reason to doubt; particularly, that where I am not understood, it shall be concluded that something very useful and profound is couched underneath; and again, that whatever word or sentence is printed in a different character shall be judged to contain something extraordinary either of wit or sublime.

As for the liberty I have thought fit to take of praising myself, upon some occasions or none, I am sure it will need no excuse if a multitude of great examples be allowed sufficient authority; for it is here to be noted that praise was originally a pension paid by the world, but the moderns, finding the trouble and charge too great in collecting it, have lately bought out the fee-simple, since which time the right of presentation is wholly in ourselves. For this reason it is that when an author makes his own eulogy, he uses a certain form to declare and insist upon his title, which is commonly in these or the like words, "I speak without vanity," which I think plainly shows it to be a matter of right and justice. Now, I do here once for all declare, that in every encounter of this nature through the following treatise the form aforesaid is implied, which I mention to save the trouble of repeating it on so many occasions.

It is a great ease to my conscience that I have written so elaborate and useful a discourse without one grain of satire intermixed, which is the sole point wherein I have taken leave to dissent from the famous originals of our age and country. I have observed some satirists to use the public much at the rate that pedants do a naughty boy ready horsed for discipline. First expostulate the case, then plead the necessity of the rod from great provocations, and conclude every period with a lash. Now, if I know anything of mankind, these gentlemen might very well spare their reproof and correction, for there is not through all Nature another so callous and insensible a member as the world's posteriors, whether you apply to it the toe or the birch. Besides, most of our late satirists seem to lie under a sort of mistake, that because nettles have the rerogative to sting, therefore all other weeds must do so too. I make not this comparison out of the least design to detract from these worthy writers, for it is well known among mythologists that weeds have the pre-eminence over all other vegetables; and therefore the first monarch of this island whose taste and judgment were so acute and refined, did very wisely root out the roses from the collar of the order and plant the thistles in their stead, as the nobler flower of the two. For which reason it is conjectured by profounder antiquaries that the satirical itch, so prevalent in this part of our island, was first brought among us from beyond the Tweed. Here may it long flourish and abound; may it survive and neglect the scorn of the world with as much ease and contempt as the world is insensible to the lashes of it. May their own dulness, or that of their party, be no discouragement for the authors to proceed; but let them remember it is with wits as with razors, which are never so apt to cut those they are employed on as when they have lost their edge. Besides, those whose teeth are too rotten to bite are best of all others qualified to revenge that defect with their breath.

I am not, like other men, to envy or undervalue the talents I cannot reach, for which reason I must needs bear a true honour to this large eminent sect of our British writers. And I hope this little panegyric will not be offensive to their ears, since it has the advantage of being only designed for themselves. Indeed, Nature herself has taken order that fame and honour should be purchased at a better pennyworth by satire than by any other productions of the brain, the world being soonest provoked to praise by lashes, as men are to love. There is a problem in an ancient author why dedications and other bundles of flattery run all upon stale musty topics, without the smallest tincture of anything new, not only to the torment and nauseating of the Christian reader, but, if not suddenly prevented, to the universal spreading of that pestilent disease the lethargy in this island, whereas there is very little satire which has not something in it untouched before. The defects of the former are usually imputed to the want of invention among those who are dealers in that kind; but I think with a great deal of injustice, the solution being easy and natural, for the materials of panegyric, being very few in number, have been long since exhausted; for as health is but one thing, and has been always the same, whereas diseases are by thousands, besides new and daily additions, so all the virtues that have been ever in mankind are to be counted upon a few fingers, but his follies and vices are innumerable, and time adds hourly to the heap. Now the utmost a poor poet can do is to get by heart a list of the cardinal virtues and deal them with his utmost liberality to his hero or his patron. He may ring the changes as far as it will go, and vary his phrase till he has talked round, but the reader quickly finds it is all pork, with a little variety of sauce, for there is no inventing terms of art beyond our ideas, and when ideas are exhausted, terms of art must be so too.

But though the matter for panegyric were as fruitful as the topics of satire, yet would it not be hard to find out a sufficient reason why the latter will be always better received than the first; for this being bestowed only upon one or a few persons at a time, is sure to raise envy, and consequently ill words, from the rest who have no share in the blessing. But satire, being levelled at all, is never resented for an offence by any, since every individual person makes bold to understand it of others, and very wisely removes his particular part of the burden upon the shoulders of the World, which are broad enough and able to bear it. To this purpose I have sometimes reflected upon the difference between Athens and England with respect to the point before us. In the Attic commonwealth it was the privilege and birthright of every citizen and poet to rail aloud and in public, or to expose upon the stage by name any person they pleased, though of the greatest figure, whether a Creon, an Hyperbolus, an Alcibiades, or a Demosthenes. But, on the other side, the least reflecting word let fall against the people in general was immediately caught up and revenged upon the authors, however considerable for their quality or their merits; whereas in England it is just the reverse of all this. Here you may securely display your utmost rhetoric against mankind in the face of the world; tell them that all are gone astray; that there is none that doeth good, no, not one; that we live in the very dregs of time; that knavery and atheism are epidemic as the pox; that honesty is fled with Astræa; with any other common-places equally new and eloquent, which are furnished by the *splendida bilis*; and when you have done, the whole audience, far from being offended, shall return you thanks as a deliverer of precious and useful truths. Nay, further, it is but to venture your lungs, and you may preach in Covent Garden against foppery and fornication, and something else; against pride, and dissimulation, and bribery at Whitehall. You may expose rapine and injustice in the Inns-of-Court chapel, and in a City pulpit be as fierce as you please against avarice, hypocrisy, and extortion. It is but a ball bandied to and fro, and every man carries a racket about him to strike it from himself among the rest of the company. But, on the other side, whoever should mistake the nature of things so far as to drop but a single hint in public how such a one starved half the fleet, and half poisoned the rest; how such a one, from a true principle of love and honour, pays no debts but for wenches and play; how such a one runs out of his estate; how Paris, bribed by Juno and Venus, loath to offend either party, slept out the whole cause on the bench; or how such an orator makes long speeches in the Senate, with much thought, little sense, and to no purpose;—whoever, I say, should venture to be thus particular, must expect to be imprisoned for *scandalum magnatum*, to have challenges sent him, to be sued for defamation, and to be brought before the bar of the House.

But I forget that I am expatiating on a subject wherein I have no concern, having neither a talent nor an inclination for satire. On the other side, I am so entirely satisfied with the whole present procedure of human things, that I have been for some years preparing material towards "A Panegyric upon the World;" to which I intended to add a second part, entitled "A Modest Defence of the Proceedings of the Rabble in all Ages." Both these I had thoughts to publish by way of appendix to the following treatise; but finding my common-place book fill much slower than I had reason to expect, I have chosen to defer them to another occasion. Besides, I have been unhappily prevented in that design by a certain domestic misfortune, in the particulars whereof, though it would be very seasonable, and much in the modern way, to inform the gentle reader, and would also be of great assistance towards extending this preface into the size now in vogue—which by rule ought to be large in proportion as the subsequent volume is small—yet I shall now dismiss our impatient reader from any further attendance at the porch; and having duly prepared his mind by a preliminary discourse, shall gladly introduce him to the sublime mysteries that ensue.

Section I

THE INTRODUCTION

Whoever has an ambition to be heard in a crowd must press, and squeeze, and thrust, and climb with indefatigable pains, till he has exalted himself to a certain degree of altitude above them. Now, in all assemblies, though you wedge them ever so close, we may observe this peculiar property, that over their heads there is room enough; but how to reach it is the difficult point, it being as hard to get quit of number as of hell.

> "—*Evadere ad auras,*
> *Hoc opus, hic labor est.*"

To this end the philosopher's way in all ages has been by erecting certain edifices in the air; but whatever practice and reputation these kind of structures have formerly possessed, or may still continue in, not excepting even that of Socrates when he was suspended in a basket to help contemplation, I think, with due submission, they seem to labour under two inconveniences. First, that the foundations being laid too high, they have been often out of sight and ever out of hearing. Secondly, that the materials being very transitory, have suffered much from inclemencies of air, especially in these north-west regions.

Therefore, towards the just performance of this great work there remain but three methods that I can think on; whereof the wisdom of our ancestors being highly sensible, has, to encourage all aspiring adventures, thought fit to erect three wooden machines for the use of those orators who desire to talk much without interruption. These are the Pulpit, the Ladder, and the Stage-itinerant. For as to the Bar, though it be compounded of the same matter and designed for the same use, it cannot, however, be well allowed the honour of a fourth, by reason of its level or inferior situation exposing it to perpetual interruption from collaterals. Neither can the Bench itself, though raised to a proper eminency, put in a better claim, whatever its advocates insist on. For if they please to look into the original design of its erection, and the circumstances or adjuncts subservient to that design, they will soon acknowledge the present practice exactly correspondent to the primitive institution, and both to answer the etymology of the name, which in the Phoenician tongue is a word of great signification, importing, if literally interpreted, "The place of sleep," but in common acceptation, "A seat well bolstered and cushioned, for the repose of old and gouty limbs;" *senes ut in otia tuta recedant.* Fortune being indebted to them this part of retaliation, that as formerly they have long talked whilst others slept, so now they may sleep as long whilst others talk.

But if no other argument could occur to exclude the Bench and the Bar from the list of oratorical machines, it were sufficient that the admission of them would overthrow a number which I was resolved to establish, whatever argument it might cost me; in imitation of that prudent method observed by many other philosophers and great clerks, whose chief art in division has been to grow fond of some proper mystical number, which their imaginations have rendered sacred to a degree that they force common reason to find room for it in every part of Nature, reducing, including, and adjusting, every genus and species within that compass by coupling some against their wills and banishing others at any rate. Now, among all the rest, the profound number THREE is that which has most employed my sublimest speculations, nor ever without wonderful delight. There is now in the press, and will be published next term, a panegyrical essay of mine upon this number, wherein I have, by most convincing proofs, not only reduced the senses and the elements under its banner, but brought over several deserters from its two great rivals, SEVEN and NINE.

Now, the first of these oratorical machines, in place as well as dignity, is the Pulpit. Of pulpits there are in this island several sorts, but I esteem only that made of timber from the Sylva Caledonia, which agrees very well with our climate. If it be upon its decay, it is the better, both for conveyance of sound and for other reasons to be mentioned by and by. The degree of perfection in shape and size I take to consist in being extremely narrow, with little ornament, and, best of all, without a cover; for, by ancient rule, it ought to be the only uncovered vessel in every assembly where it is rightfully used, by which means, from its near resemblance to a pillory, it will ever have a mighty influence on human ears.

Of Ladders I need say nothing. It is observed by foreigners themselves, to the honour of our country, that we excel all nations in our practice and understanding of this machine. The ascending orators do not only oblige their audience in the agreeable delivery, but the whole world in their early publication of their speeches, which I look upon as the choicest treasury of our British eloquence, and whereof I am informed that worthy citizen and bookseller, Mr. John Dunton, has made a faithful and a painful collection, which he shortly designs to publish in twelve volumes in folio, illustrated with copper-plates,—a work highly useful and curious, and altogether worthy of such a hand.

The last engine of orators is the Stage-itinerant, erected with much sagacity, *sub Jove pluvio, in triviis et quadriviis*. It is the great seminary of the two former, and its orators are sometimes preferred to the one and sometimes to the other, in proportion to their deservings, there being a strict and perpetual intercourse between all three.

From this accurate deduction it is manifest that for obtaining attention in public there is of necessity required a superior position of place. But although this point be generally granted, yet the cause is little agreed in; and it seems to me that very few philosophers have fallen into a true natural solution of this phenomenon. The deepest account, and the most fairly digested of any I have yet met with is this, that air being a heavy body, and therefore, according to the system of Epicurus, continually descending, must needs be more so when laden and pressed down by words, which are also bodies of much weight and gravity, as is manifest from those deep impressions they make and leave upon us, and therefore must be delivered from a due altitude, or else they will neither carry a good aim nor fall down with a sufficient force.

> *"Corpoream quoque enim vocem constare fatendum est,*
> *Et sonitum, quoniam possunt impellere sensus."*
> —*Lucr.* lib. 4.

And I am the readier to favour this conjecture from a common observation, that in the several assemblies of these orators Nature itself has instructed the hearers to stand with their mouths open and erected parallel to the horizon, so as they may be intersected by a perpendicular line from the zenith to the centre of the earth. In which position, if the audience be well compact, every one carries home a share, and little or nothing is lost.

I confess there is something yet more refined in the contrivance and structure of our modern theatres. For, first, the pit is sunk below the stage with due regard to the institution above deduced, that whatever weighty matter shall be delivered thence, whether it be lead or gold, may fall plump into the jaws of certain critics, as I think they are called, which stand ready open to devour them. Then the boxes are built round and raised to a level with the scene, in deference to the ladies, because that large portion of wit laid out in raising pruriences and protuberances is observed to run much upon a line, and ever in a circle. The whining passions and little starved conceits are gently wafted up by their own extreme levity to the middle region, and there fix and are frozen by the frigid understandings of the inhabitants. Bombast and buffoonery, by nature lofty and light, soar highest of all, and would be lost in the roof if the prudent architect had not, with much foresight, contrived for them a fourth place, called the twelve-penny gallery, and there planted a suitable colony, who greedily intercept them in their passage.

Now this physico-logical scheme of oratorical receptacles or machines contains a great mystery, being a type, a sign, an emblem, a shadow, a symbol, bearing analogy to the spacious commonwealth of writers and to those methods by which they must exalt themselves to a certain eminency above the inferior world. By the Pulpit are adumbrated the writings of our modern saints in Great Britain, as they have spiritualised and refined them from the dross and grossness of sense and human reason. The matter, as we have said, is of rotten wood, and that upon two considerations: because it is the quality of rotten wood to light in the dark; and secondly, because its cavities are full of worms—which is a type with a pair of handles, having a respect to the two principal qualifications of the orator and the two different fates attending upon his works.

The Ladder is an adequate symbol of faction and of poetry, to both of which so noble a number of authors are indebted for their fame. Of faction, because. . . (Hiatus in MS.). . . Of poetry, because its orators do *perorare* with a song; and because, climbing up by slow degrees, fate is sure to turn them off before they can reach within many steps of the top; and because it is a preferment attained by transferring of propriety and a confounding of *meum* and *tuum*.

Under the Stage-itinerant are couched those productions designed for the pleasure and delight of mortal man, such as "Six Pennyworth of Wit," "Westminster Drolleries," "Delightful Tales," "Complete Jesters," and the like, by which the writers of and for Grub Street have in these later ages so nobly triumphed over time, have clipped his wings, pared his nails, filed his teeth, turned back his hour-glass, blunted his scythe, and drawn the hobnails out of his shoes. It is under this class I have presumed to list my present treatise, being just come from having the honour conferred upon me to be adopted a member of that illustrious fraternity.

Now, I am not unaware how the productions of the Grub Street brotherhood have of late years fallen under many prejudices, nor how it has been the perpetual employment of two junior start-up societies to ridicule them and their authors as unworthy their established post in the commonwealth of wit and learning. Their own consciences will easily inform them whom I mean; nor has the world been so negligent a looker-on as not to observe the continual efforts made by the societies of Gresham and of Will's, to edify a name and reputation upon the ruin of ours. And this is yet a more feeling grief to us, upon the regards of tenderness as well as of justice, when we reflect on their proceedings not only as unjust, but as ungrateful, undutiful, and unnatural. For how can it be forgot by the world or themselves, to say nothing of our own records, which are full and clear in the point, that they both are seminaries, not only of our planting, but our watering too. I am informed our two rivals have lately made an offer to enter into the lists with united forces and challenge us to a comparison of books, both as to weight and number. In return to which, with license from our president, I humbly offer two answers. First, we say the proposal is like that which Archimedes made upon a smaller affair, including an impossibility in the practice; for where can they find scales of capacity enough for the first, or an arithmetician of capacity enough for the second. Secondly, we are ready to accept the challenge, but with this condition, that a third indifferent person be assigned, to whose impartial judgment it shall be left to decide which society each book, treatise, or pamphlet do most properly belong to. This point, God knows, is very far from being fixed at present, for we are ready to produce a catalogue of some thousands which in all common justice ought to be entitled to our fraternity, but by the revolted and newfangled writers most perfidiously ascribed to the others. Upon all which we think it very unbecoming our prudence that the determination should be remitted to the authors themselves, when our adversaries by briguing and caballing have caused so universal a defection from us, that the greatest part of our society has already deserted to them, and our nearest friends begin to stand aloof, as if they were half ashamed to own us.

This is the utmost I am authorised to say upon so ungrateful and melancholy a subject, because we are extremely unwilling to inflame a controversy whose continuance may be so fatal to the interests of us all, desiring much rather that things be amicably composed; and we shall so far advance on our side as to be ready to receive the two prodigals with open arms whenever they shall think fit to return from their husks and their harlots, which I think, from the present course of their studies, they most properly may be said to be engaged in, and, like an indulgent parent, continue to them our affection and our blessing.

But the greatest maim given to that general reception which the writings of our society have formerly received, next to the transitory state of all sublunary things, has been a superficial vein among many readers of the present age, who will by no means be persuaded to inspect beyond the surface and the rind of things; whereas wisdom is a fox, who, after long hunting, will at last cost you the pains to dig out. It is a cheese which, by how much the richer, has the thicker, the homelier, and the coarser coat, and whereof to a judicious palate the maggots are the best. It is a sack-posset, wherein the deeper you go you will find it the sweeter. Wisdom is a hen whose cackling we must value and consider, because it is attended with an egg. But then, lastly, it is a nut, which, unless you choose with judgment, may cost you a tooth, and pay you with nothing but a worm. In consequence of these momentous truths, the Grubæan sages have always chosen to convey their precepts and their arts shut up within the vehicles of types and fables; which having been perhaps more careful and curious in adorning than was altogether necessary, it has fared with these vehicles after the usual fate of coaches over-finely painted and gilt, that the transitory gazers have so dazzled their eyes and filled their imaginations with the outward lustre, as neither to regard nor consider the person or the parts of the owner within. A misfortune we undergo with somewhat less reluctancy, because it has been common to us with Pythagoras, Æsop, Socrates, and other of our predecessors.

However, that neither the world nor ourselves may any longer suffer by such misunderstandings, I have been prevailed on, after much importunity from my friends, to travail in a complete and laborious dissertation upon the prime productions of our society, which, besides their beautiful externals for the gratification of superficial readers, have darkly and deeply couched under them the most finished and refined systems of all sciences and arts, as I do not doubt to lay open by untwisting or unwinding, and either to draw up by exantlation or display by incision.

This great work was entered upon some years ago by one of our most eminent members. He began with the "History of Reynard the Fox," but neither lived to publish his essay nor to proceed farther in so useful an attempt, which is very much to be lamented, because the discovery he made and communicated to his friends is now universally received; nor do I think any of the learned will dispute that famous treatise to be a complete body of civil knowledge, and the revelation, or rather the apocalypse, of all state arcana. But the progress I have made is much greater, having already finished my annotations upon several dozens from some of which I shall impart a few hints to the candid reader, as far as will be necessary to the conclusion at which I aim.

The first piece I have handled is that of "Tom Thumb," whose author was a Pythagorean philosopher. This dark treatise contains the whole scheme of the metempsychosis, deducing the progress of the soul through all her stages.

The next is "Dr. Faustus," penned by Artephius, an author *bonæ notæ* and an adeptus; he published it in the nine hundred and eighty-fourth year of his age; this writer proceeds wholly by reincrudation, or in the *via humida*; and the marriage between Faustus and Helen does most conspicuously dilucidate the fermenting of the male and female dragon.

"Whittington and his Cat" is the work of that mysterious Rabbi, Jehuda Hannasi, containing a defence of the Gemara of the Jerusalem Misna, and its just preference to that of Babylon, contrary to the vulgar opinion.

"The Hind and Panther." This is the masterpiece of a famous writer now living, intended for a complete abstract of sixteen thousand schoolmen from Scotus to Bellarmine.

"Tommy Potts." Another piece, supposed by the same hand, by way of supplement to the former.

The "Wise Men of Gotham," *cum* Appendice. This is a treatise of immense erudition, being the great original and fountain of those arguments bandied about both in France and England, for a just defence of modern learning and wit, against the presumption, the pride, and the ignorance of the ancients. This unknown author hath so exhausted the subject, that a penetrating reader will easily discover whatever has been written since upon that dispute to be little more than repetition. An abstract of this treatise has been lately published by a worthy member of our society.

These notices may serve to give the learned reader an idea as well as a taste of what the whole work is likely to produce, wherein I have now altogether circumscribed my thoughts and my studies; and if I can bring it to a perfection before I die, shall reckon I have well employed the poor remains of an unfortunate life. This indeed is more than I can justly expect from a quill worn to the pith in the service of the State, in pros and cons upon Popish Plots, and Meal Tubs, and Exclusion Bills, and Passive Obedience, and Addresses of Lives and Fortunes; and Prerogative, and Property, and Liberty of Conscience, and Letters to a Friend: from an understanding and a conscience, threadbare and ragged with perpetual turning; from a head broken in a hundred places by the malignants of the opposite factions, and from a body spent with poxes ill cured, by trusting to bawds and surgeons, who (as it afterwards appeared) were professed enemies to me and the Government, and revenged their party's quarrel upon my nose and shins. Fourscore and eleven pamphlets have I written under three reigns, and for the service of six-and-thirty factions. But finding the State has no farther occasion for me and my ink, I retire willingly to draw it out into speculations more becoming a philosopher, having, to my unspeakable comfort, passed a long life with a conscience void of offence towards God and towards men.

But to return. I am assured from the reader's candour that the brief specimen I have given will easily clear all the rest of our society's productions from an aspersion grown, as it is manifest, out of envy and ignorance, that they are of little farther use or value to mankind beyond the common entertainments of their wit and their style; for these I am sure have never yet been disputed by our keenest adversaries; in both which, as well as the more profound and most mystical part, I have throughout this treatise closely followed the most applauded originals. And to render all complete I have with much thought and application of mind so ordered that the chief title prefixed to it (I mean that under which I design it shall pass in the common conversation of court and town) is modelled exactly after the manner peculiar to our society.

I confess to have been somewhat liberal in the business of titles, having observed the humour of multiplying them, to bear great vogue among certain writers, whom I exceedingly reverence. And indeed it seems not unreasonable that books, the children of the brain, should have the honour to be christened with variety of names, as well as other infants of quality. Our famous Dryden has ventured to proceed a point farther, endeavouring to introduce also a multiplicity of godfathers, which is an improvement of much more advantage, upon a very obvious account. It is a pity this admirable invention has not been better cultivated, so as to grow by this time into general imitation, when such an authority serves it for a precedent. Nor have my endeavours been wanting to second so useful an example, but it seems there is an unhappy expense usually annexed to the calling of a godfather, which was clearly out of my head, as it is very reasonable to believe. Where the pinch lay, I cannot certainly affirm; but having employed a world of thoughts and pains to split my treatise into forty sections, and having entreated forty Lords of my acquaintance that they would do me the honour to stand, they all made it matter of conscience, and sent me their excuses.

Section II

O nce upon a time there was a man who had three sons by one wife and all at a birth, neither could the midwife tell certainly which was the eldest. Their father died while they were young, and upon his death-bed, calling the lads to him, spoke thus:—

"Sons, because I have purchased no estate, nor was born to any, I have long considered of some good legacies to bequeath you, and at last, with much care as well as expense, have provided each of you (here they are) a new coat. Now, you are to understand that these coats have two virtues contained in them; one is, that with good wearing they will last you fresh and sound as long as you live; the other is, that they will grow in the same proportion with your bodies, lengthening and widening of themselves, so as to be always fit. Here, let me see them on you before I die. So, very well! Pray, children, wear them clean and brush them often. You will find in my will (here it is) full instructions in every particular concerning the wearing and management of your coats, wherein you must be very exact to avoid the penalties I have appointed for every transgression or neglect, upon which your future fortunes will entirely depend. I have also commanded in my will that you should live together in one house like brethren and friends, for then you will be sure to thrive and not otherwise."

Here the story says this good father died, and the three sons went all together to seek their fortunes.

I shall not trouble you with recounting what adventures they met for the first seven years, any farther than by taking notice that they carefully observed their father's will and kept their coats in very good order; that they travelled through several countries, encountered a reasonable quantity of giants, and slew certain dragons.

Being now arrived at the proper age for producing themselves, they came up to town and fell in love with the ladies, but especially three, who about that time were in chief reputation, the Duchess d'Argent, Madame de Grands-Titres, and the Countess d'Orgueil. On their first appearance, our three adventurers met with a very bad reception, and soon with great sagacity guessing out the reason, they quickly began to improve in the good qualities of the town. They wrote, and rallied, and rhymed, and sung, and said, and said nothing; they drank, and fought, and slept, and swore, and took snuff; they went to new plays on the first night, haunted the chocolate-houses, beat the watch; they bilked hackney-coachmen, ran in debt with shopkeepers, and lay with their wives; they killed bailiffs, kicked fiddlers down-stairs, ate at Locket's, loitered at Will's; they talked of the drawing-room and never came there; dined with lords they never saw; whispered a duchess and spoke never a word; exposed the scrawls of their laundress for billet-doux of quality; came ever just from court and were never seen in it; attended the levee *sub dio*; got a list of peers by heart in one company, and with great familiarity retailed them in another. Above all, they constantly attended those committees of Senators who are silent in the House and loud in the coffee-house, where they nightly adjourn to chew the cud of politics, and are encompassed with a ring of disciples who lie in wait to catch up their droppings. The three brothers had acquired forty other qualifications of the like stamp too tedious to recount, and by consequence were justly reckoned the most accomplished persons in town. But all would not suffice, and the ladies aforesaid continued still inflexible. To clear up which difficulty, I must, with the reader's good leave and patience, have recourse to some points of weight which the authors of that age have not sufficiently illustrated.

For about this time it happened a sect arose whose tenets obtained and spread very far, especially in the *grand monde*, and among everybody of good fashion. They worshipped a sort of idol, who, as their doctrine delivered, did daily create men by a kind of manufactory operation. This idol they placed in the highest parts of the house on an altar erected about three feet. He was shown in the posture of a Persian emperor sitting on a superficies with his legs interwoven under him. This god had a goose for his ensign, whence it is that some learned men pretend to deduce his original from Jupiter Capitolinus. At his left hand, beneath the altar, Hell seemed to open and catch at the animals the idol was creating, to prevent which, certain of his priests hourly flung in pieces of the uninformed mass or substance, and sometimes whole limbs already enlivened, which that horrid gulph insatiably swallowed, terrible to behold. The goose was also held a subaltern divinity or *Deus minorum gentium*, before whose shrine was sacrificed that creature whose hourly food is human gore, and who is in so great renown abroad for being the delight and favourite of the Egyptian Cercopithecus. Millions of these animals were cruelly slaughtered every day to appease the hunger of that consuming deity. The chief idol was also worshipped as the inventor of the yard and the needle, whether as the god of seamen, or on account of certain other mystical attributes, hath not been sufficiently cleared.

The worshippers of this deity had also a system of their belief which seemed to turn upon the following fundamental. They held the universe to be a large suit of clothes which invests everything; that the earth is invested by the air; the air is invested by the stars; and the stars are invested by the *Primum Mobile*. Look on this globe of earth, you will find it to be a very complete and fashionable dress. What is that which some call land but a fine coat faced with green, or the sea but a waistcoat of water-tabby? Proceed to the particular works of the creation, you will find how curious journeyman Nature hath been to trim up the vegetable beaux; observe how sparkish a periwig adorns the head of a beech, and what a fine doublet of white satin is worn by the birch. To conclude from all, what is man himself but a microcoat, or rather a complete suit of clothes with all its trimmings? As to his body there can be no dispute, but examine even the acquirements of his mind, you will find them all contribute in their order towards furnishing out an exact dress. To instance no more, is not religion a cloak, honesty a pair of shoes worn out in the dirt, self-love a surtout, vanity a shirt, and conscience a pair of breeches, which, though a cover for lewdness as well as nastiness, is easily slipped down for the service of both.

These *postulata* being admitted, it will follow in due course of reasoning that those beings which the world calls improperly suits of clothes are in reality the most refined species of animals, or to proceed higher, that they are rational creatures or men. For is it not manifest that they live, and move, and talk, and perform all other offices of human life? Are not beauty, and wit, and mien, and breeding their inseparable proprieties? In short, we see nothing but them, hear nothing but them. Is it not they who walk the streets, fill up Parliament-, coffee-, play-, bawdy-houses. It is true, indeed, that these animals, which are vulgarly called suits of clothes or dresses, do according to certain compositions receive different appellations. If one of them be trimmed up with a gold chain, and a red gown, and a white rod, and a great horse, it is called a Lord Mayor; if certain ermines and furs be placed in a certain position, we style them a judge, and so an apt conjunction of lawn and black satin we entitle a Bishop.

Others of these professors, though agreeing in the main system, were yet more refined upon certain branches of it; and held that man was an animal compounded of two dresses, the natural and the celestial suit, which were the body and the soul; that the soul was the outward, and the body the inward clothing; that the latter was *ex traduce*, but the former of daily creation and circumfusion. This last they proved by Scripture, because in them we live, and move, and have our being: as likewise by philosophy, because they are all in all, and all in every part. Besides, said they, separate these two, and you will find the body to be only a senseless unsavoury carcass. By all which it is manifest that the outward dress must needs be the soul.

To this system of religion were tagged several subaltern doctrines, which were entertained with great vogue; as particularly the faculties of the mind were deduced by the learned among them in this manner: embroidery was sheer wit, gold fringe was agreeable conversation, gold lace was repartee, a huge long periwig was humour, and a coat full of powder was very good raillery. All which required abundance of finesse and delicatesse to manage with advantage, as well as a strict observance after times and fashions.

I have with much pains and reading collected out of ancient authors this short summary of a body of philosophy and divinity which seems to have been composed by a vein and race of thinking very different from any other systems, either ancient or modern. And it was not merely to entertain or satisfy the reader's curiosity, but rather to give him light into several circumstances of the following story, that, knowing the state of dispositions and opinions in an age so remote, he may better comprehend those great events which were the issue of them. I advise, therefore, the courteous reader to peruse with a world of application, again and again, whatever I have written upon this matter. And so leaving these broken ends, I carefully gather up the chief thread of my story, and proceed.

These opinions, therefore, were so universal, as well as the practices of them, among the refined part of court and town, that our three brother adventurers, as their circumstances then stood, were strangely at a loss. For, on the one side, the three ladies they addressed themselves to (whom we have named already) were ever at the very top of the fashion, and abhorred all that were below it but the breadth of a hair. On the other side, their father's will was very precise, and it was the main precept in it, with the greatest penalties annexed, not to add to or diminish from their coats one thread without a positive command in the will. Now the coats their father had left them were, it is true, of very good cloth, and besides, so neatly sewn you would swear they were all of a piece, but, at the same time, very plain, with little or no ornament; and it happened that before they were a month in town great shoulder-knots came up. Straight all the world was shoulder-knots; no approaching the ladies' *ruelles* without the quota of shoulder-knots. "That fellow," cries one, "has no soul: where is his shoulder-knot?" Our three brethren soon discovered their want by sad experience, meeting in their walks with forty mortifications and indignities. If they went to the playhouse, the doorkeeper showed them into the twelve-penny gallery. If they called a boat, says a waterman, "I am first sculler." If they stepped into the "Rose" to take a bottle, the drawer would cry, "Friend, we sell no ale." If they went to visit a lady, a footman met them at the door with "Pray, send up your message." In this unhappy case they went immediately to consult their father's will, read it over and over, but not a word of the shoulder-knot. What should they do? What temper should they find? Obedience was absolutely necessary, and yet shoulder-knots appeared extremely requisite. After much thought, one of the brothers, who happened to be more book-learned than the other two, said he had found an expedient. "It is true," said he, "there is nothing here in this will, *totidem verbis*, making mention of shoulder-knots, but I dare conjecture we may find them inclusive, or *totidem syllabis*." This distinction was immediately approved by all; and so they fell again to examine the will. But their evil star had so directed the matter that the first syllable was not to be found in the whole writing; upon which disappointment, he who found the former evasion took heart, and said, "Brothers, there is yet hopes; for though we cannot find them *totidem verbis* nor *totidem syllabis*, I dare engage we shall make them out *tertio modo* or *totidem literis*." This discovery was also highly commended, upon which they fell once more to the scrutiny, and soon picked out S, H, O, U, L, D, E, R, when the same planet, enemy to their repose, had wonderfully contrived that a K was not to be found. Here was a weighty difficulty! But the distinguishing brother (for whom we shall hereafter find a name), now his hand was in, proved by a very good argument that K was a modern illegitimate letter, unknown to the learned ages, nor anywhere to be found in ancient manuscripts. "It is true," said he, "the word *Calendæ*, had in Q. V. C. been sometimes writ with a K, but erroneously, for in the best copies it is ever spelt with a C; and by consequence it was a gross mistake in our language to spell 'knot' with a K," but that from henceforward he would take care it should be writ with a C. Upon this all further difficulty vanished; shoulder-knots were made clearly out to be *jure paterno*, and our three gentlemen swaggered with as large and as flaunting ones as the best.

But as human happiness is of a very short duration, so in those days were human fashions, upon which it entirely depends. Shoulder-knots had their time, and we must now imagine them in their decline, for a certain lord came just from Paris with fifty yards of gold lace upon his coat, exactly trimmed after the court fashion of that month. In two days all mankind appeared closed up in bars of gold lace. Whoever durst peep abroad without his complement of gold lace was as scandalous as a —, and as ill received among the women. What should our three knights do in this momentous affair? They had sufficiently strained a point already in the affair of shoulder-knots. Upon recourse to the will, nothing appeared there but *altum silentium*. That of the shoulder-knots was a loose, flying, circumstantial point, but this of gold lace seemed too considerable an alteration without better warrant. It did *aliquo modo essentiæ adhærere*, and therefore required a positive precept. But about this time it fell out that the learned brother aforesaid had read "Aristotelis Dialectica," and especially that wonderful piece *de Interpretatione*, which has the faculty of teaching its readers to find out a meaning in everything but itself, like commentators on the Revelations, who proceed prophets without understanding a syllable of the text. "Brothers," said he, "you are to be informed that of wills, *duo sunt genera*, nuncupatory and scriptory, that in the scriptory will here before us there is no precept or mention about gold lace, *conceditur*, but *si idem affirmetur de nuncupatorio negatur*. For, brothers, if you remember, we heard a fellow say when we were boys that he heard my father's man say that he heard my father say that he would advise his sons to get gold lace on their coats as soon as ever they could procure money to buy it." "That is very true," cries the other. "I remember it perfectly well," said the third. And so, without more ado, they got the largest gold lace in the parish, and walked about as fine as lords.

A while after, there came up all in fashion a pretty sort of flame-coloured satin for linings, and the mercer brought a pattern of it immediately to our three gentlemen. "An please your worships," said he, "my Lord C— and Sir J. W. had linings out of this very piece last night; it takes wonderfully, and I shall not have a remnant left enough to make my wife a pin-cushion by to-morrow morning at ten o'clock." Upon this they fell again to rummage the will, because the present case also required a positive precept, the lining being held by orthodox writers to be of the essence of the coat. After long search they could fix upon nothing to the matter in hand, except a short advice in their father's will to take care of fire and put out their candles before they went to sleep. This, though a good deal for the purpose, and helping very far towards self-conviction, yet not seeming wholly of force to establish a command, and being resolved to avoid farther scruple, as well as future occasion for scandal, says he that was the scholar, "I remember to have read in wills of a codicil annexed, which is indeed a part of the will, and what it contains hath equal authority with the rest. Now I have been considering of this same will here before us, and I cannot reckon it to be complete for want of such a codicil. I will therefore fasten one in its proper place very dexterously. I have had it by me some time; it was written by a dog-keeper of my grandfather's, and talks a great deal, as good luck would have it, of this very flame-coloured satin." The project was immediately approved by the other two; an old parchment scroll was tagged on according to art, in the form of a codicil annexed, and the satin bought and worn.

Next winter a player, hired for the purpose by the Corporation of Fringemakers, acted his part in a new comedy, all covered with silver fringe, and according to the laudable custom gave rise to that fashion. Upon which the brothers, consulting their father's will, to their great astonishment found these words: "Item, I charge and command my said three sons to wear no sort of silver fringe upon or about their said coats," &c., with a penalty in case of disobedience too long here to insert. However, after some pause, the brother so often mentioned for his erudition, who was well skilled in criticisms, had found in a certain author, which he said should be nameless, that the same word which in the will is called fringe does also signify a broom-stick, and doubtless ought to have the same interpretation in this paragraph. This another of the brothers disliked, because of that epithet silver, which could not, he humbly conceived, in propriety of speech be reasonably applied to a broom-stick; but it was replied upon him that this epithet was understood in a mythological and allegorical sense. However, he objected again why their father should forbid them to wear a broom-stick on their coats, a caution that seemed unnatural and impertinent; upon which he was taken up short, as one that spoke irreverently of a mystery which doubtless was very useful and significant, but ought not to be over-curiously pried into or nicely reasoned upon. And in short, their father's authority being now considerably sunk, this expedient was allowed to serve as a lawful dispensation for wearing their full proportion of silver fringe.

A while after was revived an old fashion, long antiquated, of embroidery with Indian figures of men, women, and children. Here they had no occasion to examine the will. They remembered but too well how their father had always abhorred this fashion; that he made several paragraphs on purpose, importing his utter detestation of it, and bestowing his everlasting curse to his sons whenever they should wear it. For all this, in a few days they appeared higher in the fashion than anybody else in the town. But they solved the matter by saying that these figures were not at all the same with those that were formerly worn and were meant in the will; besides, they did not wear them in that sense, as forbidden by their father, but as they were a commendable custom, and of great use to the public. That these rigorous clauses in the will did therefore require some allowance and a favourable interpretation, and ought to be understood *cum grano salis*.

But fashions perpetually altering in that age, the scholastic brother grew weary of searching further evasions and solving everlasting contradictions. Resolved, therefore, at all hazards to comply with the modes of the world, they concerted matters together, and agreed unanimously to lock up their father's will in a strong-box, brought out of Greece or Italy (I have forgot which), and trouble themselves no farther to examine it, but only refer to its authority whenever they thought fit. In consequence whereof, a while after it grew a general mode to wear an infinite number of points, most of them tagged with silver; upon which the scholar pronounced *ex cathedrâ* that points were absolutely *jure paterno* as they might very well remember. It is true, indeed, the fashion prescribed somewhat more than were directly named in the will; however, that they, as heirs-general of their father, had power to make and add certain clauses for public emolument, though not deducible *todidem verbis* from the letter of the will, or else *multa absurda sequerentur*. This was understood for canonical, and therefore on the following Sunday they came to church all covered with points.

The learned brother so often mentioned was reckoned the best scholar in all that or the next street to it; insomuch, as having run something behindhand with the world, he obtained the favour from a certain lord to receive him into his house and to teach his children. A while after the lord died, and he, by long practice upon his father's will, found the way of contriving a deed of conveyance of that house to himself and his heirs; upon which he took possession, turned the young squires out, and received his brothers in their stead.

JONATHAN SWIFT

Section III

A Digression Concerning Critics

Though I have been hitherto as cautious as I could, upon all occasions, most nicely to follow the rules and methods of writing laid down by the example of our illustrious moderns, yet has the unhappy shortness of my memory led me into an error, from which I must immediately extricate myself, before I can decently pursue my principal subject. I confess with shame it was an unpardonable omission to proceed so far as I have already done before I had performed the due discourses, expostulatory, supplicatory, or deprecatory, with my good lords the critics. Towards some atonement for this grievous neglect, I do here make humbly bold to present them with a short account of themselves and their art, by looking into the original and pedigree of the word, as it is generally understood among us, and very briefly considering the ancient and present state thereof.

By the word critic, at this day so frequent in all conversations, there have sometimes been distinguished three very different species of mortal men, according as I have read in ancient books and pamphlets. For first, by this term were understood such persons as invented or drew up rules for themselves and the world, by observing which a careful reader might be able to pronounce upon the productions of the learned, form his taste to a true relish of the sublime and the admirable, and divide every beauty of matter or of style from the corruption that apes it. In their common perusal of books, singling out the errors and defects, the nauseous, the fulsome, the dull, and the impertinent, with the caution of a man that walks through Edinburgh streets in a morning, who is indeed as careful as he can to watch diligently and spy out the filth in his way; not that he is curious to observe the colour and complexion of the ordure or take its dimensions, much less to be paddling in or tasting it, but only with a design to come out as cleanly as he may. These men seem, though very erroneously, to have understood the appellation of critic in a literal sense; that one principal part of his office was to praise and acquit, and that a critic who sets up to read only for an occasion of censure and reproof is a creature as barbarous as a judge who should take up a resolution to hang all men that came before him upon a trial.

Again, by the word critic have been meant the restorers of ancient learning from the worms, and graves, and dust of manuscripts.

Now the races of these two have been for some ages utterly extinct, and besides to discourse any further of them would not be at all to my purpose.

The third and noblest sort is that of the true critic, whose original is the most ancient of all. Every true critic is a hero born, descending in a direct line from a celestial stem, by Momus and Hybris, who begat Zoilus, who begat Tigellius, who begat Etcætera the elder, who begat Bentley, and Rymer, and Wotton, and Perrault, and Dennis, who begat Etcætera the younger.

And these are the critics from whom the commonwealth of learning has in all ages received such immense benefits, that the gratitude of their admirers placed their origin in heaven, among those of Hercules, Theseus, Perseus, and other great deservers of mankind. But heroic virtue itself hath not been exempt from the obloquy of evil tongues. For it hath been objected that those ancient heroes, famous for their combating so many giants, and dragons, and robbers, were in their own persons a greater nuisance to mankind than any of those monsters they subdued; and therefore, to render their obligations more complete, when all other vermin were destroyed, should in conscience have concluded with the same justice upon themselves, as Hercules most generously did, and hath upon that score procured for himself more temples and votaries than the best of his fellows. For these reasons I suppose it is why some have conceived it would be very expedient for the public good of learning that every true critic, as soon as he had finished his task assigned, should immediately deliver himself up to ratsbane or hemp, or from some convenient altitude, and that no man's pretensions to so illustrious a character should by any means be received before that operation was performed.

Now, from this heavenly descent of criticism, and the close analogy it bears to heroic virtue, it is easy to assign the proper employment of a true, ancient, genuine critic: which is, to travel through this vast world of writings; to peruse and hunt those monstrous faults bred within them; to drag out the lurking errors, like Cacus from his den; to multiply them like Hydra's heads; and rake them together like Augeas's dung; or else to drive away a sort of dangerous fowl who have a perverse inclination to plunder the best branches of the tree of knowledge, like those Stymphalian birds that ate up the fruit.

These reasonings will furnish us with an adequate definition of a true critic: that he is a discoverer and collector of writers' faults; which may be further put beyond dispute by the following demonstration:— That whoever will examine the writings in all kinds wherewith this ancient sect hath honoured the world, shall immediately find from the whole thread and tenor of them that the ideas of the authors have been altogether conversant and taken up with the faults, and blemishes, and oversights, and mistakes of other writers, and let the subject treated on be whatever it will, their imaginations are so entirely possessed and replete with the defects of other pens, that the very quintessence of what is bad does of necessity distil into their own, by which means the whole appears to be nothing else but an abstract of the criticisms themselves have made.

Having thus briefly considered the original and office of a critic, as the word is understood in its most noble and universal acceptation, I proceed to refute the objections of those who argue from the silence and pretermission of authors, by which they pretend to prove that the very art of criticism, as now exercised, and by me explained, is wholly modern, and consequently that the critics of Great Britain and France have no title to an original so ancient and illustrious as I have deduced. Now, if I can clearly make out, on the contrary, that the most ancient writers have particularly described both the person and the office of a true critic agreeable to the definition laid down by me, their grand objection—from the silence of authors—will fall to the ground.

I confess to have for a long time borne a part in this general error, from which I should never have acquitted myself but through the assistance of our noble moderns, whose most edifying volumes I turn indefatigably over night and day, for the improvement of my mind and the good of my country. These have with unwearied pains made many useful searches into the weak sides of the ancients, and given us a comprehensive list of them. Besides, they have proved beyond contradiction that the very finest things delivered of old have been long since invented and brought to light by much later pens, and that the noblest discoveries those ancients ever made in art or nature have all been produced by the transcending genius of the present age, which clearly shows how little merit those ancients can justly pretend to, and takes off that blind admiration paid them by men in a corner, who have the unhappiness of conversing too little with present things. Reflecting maturely upon all this, and taking in the whole compass of human nature, I easily concluded that these ancients, highly sensible of their many imperfections, must needs have endeavoured, from some passages in their works, to obviate, soften, or divert the censorious reader, by satire or panegyric upon the true critics, in imitation of their masters, the moderns. Now, in the commonplaces of both these I was plentifully instructed by a long course of useful study in prefaces and prologues, and therefore immediately resolved to try what I could discover of either, by a diligent perusal of the most ancient writers, and especially those who treated of the earliest times.

Here I found, to my great surprise, that although they all entered upon occasion into particular descriptions of the true critic, according as they were governed by their fears or their hopes, yet whatever they touched of that kind was with abundance of caution, adventuring no further than mythology and hieroglyphic. This, I suppose, gave ground to superficial readers for urging the silence of authors against the antiquity of the true critic, though the types are so apposite, and the applications so necessary and natural, that it is not easy to conceive how any reader of modern eye and taste could overlook them. I shall venture from a great number to produce a few which I am very confident will put this question beyond doubt.

It well deserves considering that these ancient writers, in treating enigmatically upon this subject, have generally fixed upon the very same hieroglyph, varying only the story according to their affections or their wit. For first, Pausanias is of opinion that the perfection of writing correct was entirely owing to the institution of critics, and that he can possibly mean no other than the true critic is, I think, manifest enough from the following description. He says they were a race of men who delighted to nibble at the superfluities and excrescences of books, which the learned at length observing, took warning of their own accord to lop the luxuriant, the rotten, the dead, the sapless, and the overgrown branches from their works. But now all this he cunningly shades under the following allegory: That the Nauplians in Argia learned the art of pruning their vines by observing that when an ass had browsed upon one of them, it thrived the better and bore fairer fruit. But Herodotus holding the very same hieroglyph, speaks much plainer and almost *in terminis*. He hath been so bold as to tax the true critics of ignorance and malice, telling us openly, for I think nothing can be plainer, that in the western part of Libya there were asses with horns, upon which relation Ctesias yet refines, mentioning the very same animal about

India; adding, that whereas all other asses wanted a gall, these horned ones were so redundant in that part that their flesh was not to be eaten because of its extreme bitterness.

Now, the reason why those ancient writers treated this subject only by types and figures was because they durst not make open attacks against a party so potent and so terrible as the critics of those ages were, whose very voice was so dreadful that a legion of authors would tremble and drop their pens at the sound. For so Herodotus tells us expressly in another place how a vast army of Scythians was put to flight in a panic terror by the braying of an ass. From hence it is conjectured by certain profound philologers, that the great awe and reverence paid to a true critic by the writers of Britain have been derived to us from those our Scythian ancestors. In short, this dread was so universal, that in process of time those authors who had a mind to publish their sentiments more freely in describing the true critics of their several ages, were forced to leave off the use of the former hieroglyph as too nearly approaching the prototype, and invented other terms instead thereof that were more cautious and mystical. So Diodorus, speaking to the same purpose, ventures no farther than to say that in the mountains of Helicon there grows a certain weed which bears a flower of so damned a scent as to poison those who offer to smell it. Lucretius gives exactly the same relation.

> *"Est etiam in magnis Heliconis montibus arbos,*
> *Floris odore hominem retro consueta necare."*
>
> —*Lib.* 6.

But Ctesias, whom we lately quoted, has been a great deal bolder; he had been used with much severity by the true critics of his own age, and therefore could not forbear to leave behind him at least one deep mark of his vengeance against the whole tribe. His meaning is so near the surface that I wonder how it possibly came to be overlooked by those who deny the antiquity of the true critics. For pretending to make a description of many strange animals about India, he has set down these remarkable words. "Among the rest," says he, "there is a serpent that wants teeth, and consequently cannot bite, but if its vomit (to which it is much addicted) happens to fall upon anything, a certain rottenness or corruption ensues. These serpents are generally found among the mountains where jewels grow, and they frequently emit a poisonous juice, whereof whoever drinks, that person's brain flies out of his nostrils."

There was also among the ancients a sort of critic, not distinguished in specie from the former but in growth or degree, who seem to have been only the tyros or junior scholars, yet because of their differing employments they are frequently mentioned as a sect by themselves. The usual exercise of these young students was to attend constantly at theatres, and learn to spy out the worst parts of the play, whereof they were obliged carefully to take note, and render a rational account to their tutors. Fleshed at these smaller sports, like young wolves, they grew up in time to be nimble and strong enough for hunting down large game. For it has been observed, both among ancients and moderns, that a true critic has one quality in common with a whore and an alderman, never to change his title or his nature; that a grey critic has been certainly a green one, the perfections and acquirements of his age being only the improved talents of his youth, like hemp, which some naturalists inform us is bad for suffocations, though taken but in the seed. I esteem the invention, or at least the refinement of prologues, to have been owing to these younger proficients, of whom Terence makes frequent and honourable mention, under the name of Malevoli.

Now it is certain the institution of the true critics was of absolute necessity to the commonwealth of learning. For all human actions seem to be divided like Themistocles and his company. One man can fiddle, and another can make a small town a great city; and he that cannot do either one or the other deserves to be kicked out of the creation. The avoiding of which penalty has doubtless given the first birth to the nation of critics, and withal an occasion for their secret detractors to report that a true critic is a sort of mechanic set up with a stock and tools for his trade, at as little expense as a tailor; and that there is much analogy between the utensils and abilities of both. That the "Tailor's Hell" is the type of a critic's commonplace-book, and his wit and learning held forth by the goose. That it requires at least as many of these to the making up of one scholar as of the others to the composition of a man. That the valour of both is equal, and their weapons near of a size. Much may be said in answer to these invidious reflections; and I can positively affirm the first to be a falsehood: for, on the contrary, nothing is more certain than that it requires greater layings out to be free of the critic's company than of any other you can name. For as to be a true beggar, it will cost the richest candidate every groat he is worth, so before one can commence a true critic, it will cost a man all the good qualities of his mind, which perhaps for a less purchase would be thought but an indifferent bargain.

Having thus amply proved the antiquity of criticism and described the primitive state of it, I shall now examine the present condition of this Empire, and show how well it agrees with its ancient self. A certain author, whose works have many ages since been entirely lost, does in his fifth book and eighth chapter say of critics that "their writings are the mirrors of learning." This I understand in a literal sense, and suppose our author must mean that whoever designs to be a perfect writer must inspect into the books of critics, and correct his inventions there as in a mirror. Now, whoever considers that the mirrors of the ancients were made of brass and fine mercurio, may presently apply the two principal qualifications of a true modern critic, and consequently must needs conclude that these have always been and must be for ever the same. For brass is an emblem of duration, and when it is skilfully burnished will cast reflections from its own superficies without any assistance of mercury from behind. All the other talents of a critic will not require a particular mention, being included or easily deducible to these. However, I shall conclude with three maxims, which may serve both as characteristics to distinguish a true modern critic from a pretender, and will be also of admirable use to those worthy spirits who engage in so useful and honourable an art.

The first is, that criticism, contrary to all other faculties of the intellect, is ever held the truest and best when it is the very first result of the critic's mind; as fowlers reckon the first aim for the surest, and seldom fail of missing the mark if they stay not for a second.

Secondly, the true critics are known by their talent of swarming about the noblest writers, to which they are carried merely by instinct, as a rat to the best cheese, or a wasp to the fairest fruit. So when the king is a horseback he is sure to be the dirtiest person of the company, and they that make their court best are such as bespatter him most.

Lastly, a true critic in the perusal of a book is like a dog at a feast, whose thoughts and stomach are wholly set upon what the guests fling away, and consequently is apt to snarl most when there are the fewest bones.

Thus much I think is sufficient to serve by way of address to my patrons, the true modern critics, and may very well atone for my past silence, as well as that which I am like to observe for the future. I hope I have deserved so well of their whole body as to meet with generous and tender usage at their hands. Supported by which expectation I go on boldly to pursue those adventures already so happily begun.

Section IV

A Tale of a Tub

I have now with much pains and study conducted the reader to a period where he must expect to hear of great revolutions. For no sooner had our learned brother, so often mentioned, got a warm house of his own over his head, than he began to look big and to take mightily upon him, insomuch that unless the gentle reader out of his great candour will please a little to exalt his idea, I am afraid he will henceforth hardly know the hero of the play when he happens to meet him, his part, his dress, and his mien being so much altered.

He told his brothers he would have them to know that he was their elder, and consequently his father's sole heir; nay, a while after, he would not allow them to call him brother, but Mr. Peter; and then he must be styled Father Peter, and sometimes My Lord Peter. To support this grandeur, which he soon began to consider could not be maintained without a better *fonde* than what he was born to, after much thought he cast about at last to turn projector and virtuoso, wherein he so well succeeded, that many famous discoveries, projects, and machines which bear great vogue and practice at present in the world, are owing entirely to Lord Peter's invention. I will deduce the best account I have been able to collect of the chief amongst them, without considering much the order they came out in, because I think authors are not well agreed as to that point.

I hope when this treatise of mine shall be translated into foreign languages (as I may without vanity affirm that the labour of collecting, the faithfulness in recounting, and the great usefulness of the matter to the public, will amply deserve that justice), that of the several Academies abroad, especially those of France and Italy, will favourably accept these humble offers for the advancement of universal knowledge. I do also advertise the most reverend fathers the Eastern missionaries that I have purely for their sakes made use of such words and phrases as will best admit an easy turn into any of the Oriental languages, especially the Chinese. And so I proceed with great content of mind upon reflecting how much emolument this whole globe of earth is like to reap by my labours.

The first undertaking of Lord Peter was to purchase a large continent, lately said to have been discovered in *Terra Australis incognita*. This tract of land he bought at a very great pennyworth from the discoverers themselves (though some pretended to doubt whether they had ever been there), and then retailed it into several cantons to certain dealers, who carried over colonies, but were all shipwrecked in the voyage; upon which Lord Peter sold the said continent to other customers again and again, and again and again, with the same success.

The second project I shall mention was his sovereign remedy for the worms, especially those in the spleen. The patient was to eat nothing after supper for three nights; as soon as he went to bed, he was carefully to lie on one side, and when he grew weary, to turn upon the other. He must also duly confine his two eyes to the same object, and by no means break wind at both ends together without manifest occasion. These prescriptions diligently observed, the worms would void insensibly by perspiration ascending through the brain.

A third invention was the erecting of a whispering-office for the public good and ease of all such as are hypochondriacal or troubled with the cholic, as likewise of all eavesdroppers, physicians, midwives, small politicians, friends fallen out, repeating poets, lovers happy or in despair, bawds, privy-counsellors, pages, parasites and buffoons, in short, of all such as are in danger of bursting with too much wind. An ass's head was placed so conveniently, that the party affected might easily with his mouth accost either of the animal's ears, which he was to apply close for a certain space, and by a fugitive faculty peculiar to the ears of that animal, receive immediate benefit, either by eructation, or expiration, or evomition.

Another very beneficial project of Lord Peter's was an office of insurance for tobacco-pipes, martyrs of the modern zeal, volumes of poetry, shadows. . . and rivers, that these, nor any of these, shall receive damage by fire. From whence our friendly societies may plainly find themselves to be only transcribers from this original, though the one and the other have been of great benefit to the undertakers as well as of equal to the public.

Lord Peter was also held the original author of puppets and raree-shows, the great usefulness whereof being so generally known, I shall not enlarge farther upon this particular.

But another discovery for which he was much renowned was his famous universal pickle. For having remarked how your common pickle in use among housewives was of no farther benefit than to preserve dead flesh and certain kinds of vegetables, Peter with great cost as well as art had contrived a pickle proper for houses, gardens, towns, men, women, children, and cattle, wherein he could preserve them as sound as insects in amber. Now this pickle to the taste, the smell, and the sight, appeared exactly the same with what is in common service for beef, and butter, and herrings (and has been often that way applied with great success), but for its many sovereign virtues was quite a different thing. For Peter would put in a certain quantity of his powder pimperlim-pimp, after which it never failed of success. The operation was performed by spargefaction in a proper time of the moon. The patient who was to be pickled, if it were a house, would infallibly be preserved from all spiders, rats, and weasels; if the party affected were a dog, he should be exempt from mange, and madness, and hunger. It also infallibly took away all scabs and lice, and scalled heads from children, never hindering the patient from any duty, either at bed or board.

But of all Peter's rarities, he most valued a certain set of bulls, whose race was by great fortune preserved in a lineal descent from those that guarded the golden-fleece. Though some who pretended to observe them curiously doubted the breed had not been kept entirely chaste, because they had degenerated from their ancestors in some qualities, and had acquired others very extraordinary, but a foreign mixture. The bulls of Colchis are recorded to have brazen feet; but whether it happened by ill pasture and running, by an alloy from intervention of other parents from stolen intrigues; whether a weakness in their progenitors had impaired the seminal virtue, or by a decline necessary through a long course of time, the originals of nature being depraved in these latter sinful ages of the world—whatever was the cause, it is certain that Lord Peter's bulls were extremely vitiated by the rust of time in the metal of their feet, which was now sunk into common lead. However, the terrible roaring peculiar to their lineage was preserved, as likewise that faculty of breathing out fire from their nostrils; which notwithstanding many of their detractors took to be a feat of art, and to be nothing so terrible as it appeared, proceeding only from their usual course of diet, which was of squibs and crackers. However, they had two peculiar marks which extremely distinguished them from the bulls of Jason, and which I have not met together in the description of any other monster beside that in Horace, "Varias inducere plumas," and "Atrum definit in piscem." For these had fishes tails, yet upon occasion could outfly any bird in the air. Peter put these bulls upon several employs. Sometimes he would set them a roaring to fright naughty boys and make them quiet. Sometimes he would send them out upon errands of great importance, where it is wonderful to recount, and perhaps the cautious reader may think much to believe it; an *appetitus sensibilis* deriving itself through the whole family from their noble ancestors, guardians of the Golden Fleece, they continued so extremely fond of gold, that if Peter sent them abroad, though it were only upon a compliment, they would roar, and spit, and belch, and snivel out fire, and keep a perpetual coil till you flung them a bit of gold; but then *pulveris exigui jactu*, they would grow calm and quiet as lambs. In short, whether by secret connivance or encouragement from their master, or out of their own liquorish affection to gold, or both, it is certain they were no better than a sort of sturdy, swaggering beggars; and where they could not prevail to get an alms, would make women miscarry and children fall into fits; who to this very day usually call sprites and hobgoblins by the name of bull-beggars. They grew at last so very troublesome to the neighbourhood, that some gentlemen of the North-West got a parcel of right English bull-dogs, and baited them so terribly, that they felt it ever after.

I must needs mention one more of Lord Peter's projects, which was very extraordinary, and discovered him to be master of a high reach and profound invention. Whenever it happened that any rogue of Newgate was condemned to be hanged, Peter would offer him a pardon for a certain sum of money, which when the poor caitiff had made all shifts to scrape up and send, his lordship would return a piece of paper in this form:—

"To all mayors, sheriffs, jailors, constables, bailiffs, hangmen, &c. Whereas we are informed that A. B. remains in the hands of you, or any of you, under the sentence of death. We will and command you, upon sight hereof, to let the said prisoner depart to his own habitation, whether he stands condemned for murder, sodomy, rape, sacrilege, incest, treason, blasphemy, &c., for which this shall be your sufficient warrant. And if you fail hereof, G— d—mn you and yours to all eternity. And so we bid you heartily farewell. Your most humble man's man,

EMPEROR PETER

The wretches trusting to this lost their lives and money too.

I desire of those whom the learned among posterity will appoint for commentators upon this elaborate treatise, that they will proceed with great caution upon certain dark points, wherein all who are not *verè adepti* may be in danger to form rash and hasty conclusions, especially in some mysterious paragraphs, where certain arcana are joined for brevity sake, which in the operation must be divided. And I am certain that future sons of art will return large thanks to my memory for so grateful, so useful an inmuendo.

It will be no difficult part to persuade the reader that so many worthy discoveries met with great success in the world; though I may justly assure him that I have related much the smallest number; my design having been only to single out such as will be of most benefit for public imitation, or which best served to give some idea of the reach and wit of the inventor. And therefore it need not be wondered if by this time Lord Peter was become exceeding rich. But alas! he had kept his brain so long and so violently upon the rack, that at last it shook itself, and began to turn round for a little ease. In short, what with pride, projects, and knavery, poor Peter was grown distracted, and conceived the strangest imaginations in the world. In the height of his fits (as it is usual with those who run mad out of pride) he would call himself God Almighty, and sometimes monarch of the universe. I have seen him (says my author) take three old high-crowned hats, and clap them all on his head, three storey high, with a huge bunch of keys at his girdle, and an angling rod in his hand. In which guise, whoever went to take him by the hand in the way of salutation, Peter with much grace, like a well-educated spaniel, would present them with his foot, and if they refused his civility, then he would raise it as high as their chops, and give them a damned kick on the mouth, which hath ever since been called a salute. Whoever walked by without paying him their compliments, having a wonderful strong breath, he would blow their hats off into the dirt. Meantime his affairs at home went upside down, and his two brothers had a wretched time, where his first *boutade* was to kick both their wives one morning out of doors, and his own too, and in their stead gave orders to pick up the first three strollers could be met with in the streets. A while after he nailed up the cellar door, and would not allow his brothers a drop of drink to their victuals. Dining one day at an alderman's in the city, Peter observed him expatiating, after the manner of his brethren in the praises of his sirloin of beef. "Beef," said the sage magistrate, "is the king of meat; beef comprehends in it the quintessence of partridge, and quail, and venison, and pheasant, and plum-pudding, and custard." When Peter came home, he would needs take the fancy of cooking up this doctrine into use, and apply the precept in default of a sirloin to his brown loaf. "Bread," says he, "dear brothers, is the staff of life, in which bread is contained inclusive the quintessence of beef, mutton, veal, venison, partridge, plum-pudding, and custard, and to render all complete, there is intermingled a due quantity of water, whose crudities are also corrected by yeast or barm, through which means it becomes a wholesome fermented liquor, diffused through the mass of the bread." Upon the strength of these conclusions, next day at dinner was the brown loaf served up in all the formality of a City feast. "Come, brothers," said Peter, "fall to, and spare not; here is excellent good mutton; or hold, now my hand is in, I'll help you." At which word, in much ceremony, with fork and knife, he carves out two good slices of a loaf, and presents each on a plate to his brothers. The elder of the two, not suddenly entering into Lord Peter's conceit, began with very civil language to examine the mystery. "My lord," said he, "I doubt, with great submission, there may be some mistake." "What!" says Peter, "you are pleasant; come then, let us hear this jest your head is so big with." "None in the world, my Lord; but unless I am very much deceived, your Lordship was pleased a while ago to let fall a word about mutton, and I would be glad to see it with all my heart." "How," said Peter, appearing in great surprise, "I do not comprehend this at all;" upon which the younger, interposing to set the business right, "My Lord," said he, "my brother, I suppose, is hungry, and longs for the mutton your Lordship hath promised us to dinner." "Pray," said Peter, "take me along with you, either you are both mad, or disposed to be merrier than I approve of; if you there do not like your piece, I will carve you another, though I should take that to be the choice bit of the whole shoulder." "What then, my Lord?" replied the first; "it seems this is a shoulder of mutton all this while." "Pray, sir," says Peter, "eat your victuals and leave off your impertinence, if you please, for I am not disposed to relish it at present;" but the other could not forbear, being over-provoked at the affected seriousness of Peter's countenance. "My Lord," said he, "I can only say, that to my eyes and fingers, and teeth and nose, it seems to be nothing but a crust of bread." Upon which the second put in his word. "I never saw a piece of mutton in my life so nearly resembling a slice from a twelve-penny loaf." "Look ye, gentlemen," cries Peter in a rage, "to convince you what a couple of blind, positive, ignorant, wilful puppies you are, I will use but this plain argument; by G—, it is true, good, natural mutton as any in Leadenhall Market; and

G— confound you both eternally if you offer to believe otherwise." Such a thundering proof as this left no further room for objection; the two unbelievers began to gather and pocket up their mistake as hastily as they could. "Why, truly," said the first, "upon more mature consideration"— "Ay," says the other, interrupting him, "now I have thought better on the thing, your Lordship seems to have a great deal of reason." "Very well," said Peter. "Here, boy, fill me a beer-glass of claret. Here's to you both with all my heart." The two brethren, much delighted to see him so readily appeased, returned their most humble thanks, and said they would be glad to pledge his Lordship. "That you shall," said Peter, "I am not a person to refuse you anything that is reasonable; wine moderately taken is a cordial. Here is a glass apiece for you; it is true natural juice from the grape; none of your damned vintner's brewings." Having spoke thus, he presented to each of them another large dry crust, bidding them drink it off, and not be bashful, for it would do them no hurt. The two brothers, after having performed the usual office in such delicate conjunctures, of staring a sufficient period at Lord Peter and each other, and finding how matters were like to go, resolved not to enter on a new dispute, but let him carry the point as he pleased; for he was now got into one of his mad fits, and to argue or expostulate further would only serve to render him a hundred times more untractable.

I have chosen to relate this worthy matter in all its circumstances, because it gave a principal occasion to that great and famous rupture which happened about the same time among these brethren, and was never afterwards made up. But of that I shall treat at large in another section.

However, it is certain that Lord Peter, even in his lucid intervals, was very lewdly given in his common conversation, extreme wilful and positive, and would at any time rather argue to the death than allow himself to be once in an error. Besides, he had an abominable faculty of telling huge palpable lies upon all occasions, and swearing not only to the truth, but cursing the whole company to hell if they pretended to make the least scruple of believing him. One time he swore he had a cow at home which gave as much milk at a meal as would fill three thousand churches, and what was yet more extraordinary, would never turn sour. Another time he was telling of an old sign-post that belonged to his father, with nails and timber enough on it to build sixteen large men-of-war. Talking one day of Chinese waggons, which were made so light as to sail over mountains, "Z—nds," said Peter, "where's the wonder of that? By G—, I saw a large house of lime and stone travel over sea and land (granting that it stopped sometimes to bait) above two thousand German leagues." And that which was the good of it, he would swear desperately all the while that he never told a lie in his life, and at every word: "By G— gentlemen, I tell you nothing but the truth, and the d—l broil them eternally that will not believe me."

In short, Peter grew so scandalous that all the neighbourhood began in plain words to say he was no better than a knave; and his two brothers, long weary of his ill-usage, resolved at last to leave him; but first they humbly desired a copy of their father's will, which had now lain by neglected time out of mind. Instead of granting this request, he called them rogues, traitors, and the rest of the vile names he could muster up. However, while he was abroad one day upon his projects, the two youngsters watched their opportunity, made a shift to come at the will, and took a *copia vera*, by which they presently saw how grossly they had been abused, their father having left them equal heirs, and strictly commanded that whatever they got should lie in common among them all. Pursuant to which, their next enterprise was to break open the cellar-door and get a little good drink to spirit and comfort their hearts. In copying the will, they had met another precept against whoring, divorce, and separate maintenance; upon which, their next work was to discard their concubines and send for their wives. Whilst all this was in agitation, there enters a solicitor from Newgate, desiring Lord Peter would please to procure a pardon for a thief that was to be hanged to-morrow. But the two brothers told him he was a coxcomb to seek pardons from a fellow who deserved to be hanged much better than his client, and discovered all the method of that imposture in the same form I delivered it a while ago, advising the solicitor to put his friend upon obtaining a pardon from the king. In the midst of all this platter and revolution in comes Peter with a file of dragoons at his heels, and gathering from all hands what was in the wind, he and his gang, after several millions of scurrilities and curses not very important here to repeat, by main force very fairly kicks them both out of doors, and would never let them come under his roof from that day to this.

Section V

A Digression in the Modern Kind

W e whom the world is pleased to honour with the title of modern authors, should never have been able to compass our great design of an everlasting remembrance and never-dying fame if our endeavours had not been so highly serviceable to the general good of mankind. This, O universe! is the adventurous attempt of me, thy secretary—

> *"Quemvis perferre laborem*
> *Suadet, et inducit noctes vigilare serenas."*

To this end I have some time since, with a world of pains and art, dissected the carcass of human nature, and read many useful lectures upon the several parts, both containing and contained, till at last it smelt so strong I could preserve it no longer. Upon which I have been at a great expense to fit up all the bones with exact contexture and in due symmetry, so that I am ready to show a very complete anatomy thereof to all curious gentlemen and others. But not to digress further in the midst of a digression, as I have known some authors enclose digressions in one another like a nest of boxes, I do affirm that, having carefully cut up human nature, I have found a very strange, new, and important discovery: that the public good of mankind is performed by two ways—instruction and diversion. And I have further proved my said several readings (which, perhaps, the world may one day see, if I can prevail on any friend to steal a copy, or on certain gentlemen of my admirers to be very importunate) that, as mankind is now disposed, he receives much greater advantage by being diverted than instructed, his epidemical diseases being fastidiosity, amorphy, and oscitation; whereas, in the present universal empire of wit and learning, there seems but little matter left for instruction. However, in compliance with a lesson of great age and authority, I have attempted carrying the point in all its heights, and accordingly throughout this divine treatise have skilfully kneaded up both together with a layer of *utile* and a layer of *dulce*.

When I consider how exceedingly our illustrious moderns have eclipsed the weak glimmering lights of the ancients, and turned them out of the road of all fashionable commerce to a degree that our choice town wits of most refined accomplishments are in grave dispute whether there have been ever any ancients or no; in which point we are like to receive wonderful satisfaction from the most useful labours and lucubrations of that worthy modern, Dr. Bentley. I say, when I consider all this, I cannot but bewail that no famous modern hath ever yet attempted an universal system in a small portable volume of all things that are to be known, or believed, or imagined, or practised in life. I am, however, forced to acknowledge that such an enterprise was thought on some time ago by a great philosopher of O-Brazile. The method he proposed was by a certain curious receipt, a nostrum, which after his untimely death I found among his papers, and do here, out of my great affection to the modern learned, present them with it, not doubting it may one day encourage some worthy undertaker.

You take fair correct copies, well bound in calf's skin and lettered at the back, of all modern bodies of arts and sciences whatsoever, and in what language you please. These you distil in *balneo Mariæ*, infusing quintessence of poppy Q.S., together with three pints of lethe, to be had from the apothecaries. You cleanse away carefully the *sordes* and *caput mortuum*, letting all that is volatile evaporate. You preserve only the first running, which is again to be distilled seventeen times, till what remains will amount to about two drams. This you keep in a glass vial hermetically sealed for one-and-twenty days. Then you begin your catholic treatise, taking every morning fasting (first shaking the vial) three drops of this elixir, snuffing it strongly up your nose. It will dilate itself about the brain (where there is any) in fourteen minutes, and you immediately perceive in your head an infinite number of abstracts, summaries, compendiums, extracts, collections, medullas, excerpta quædams, florilegias and the like, all disposed into great order and reducible upon paper.

I must needs own it was by the assistance of this arcanum that I, though otherwise *impar*, have adventured upon so daring an attempt, never achieved or undertaken before but by a certain author called Homer, in whom, though otherwise a person not without some abilities, and for an ancient of a tolerable genius; I have discovered many gross errors which are not to be forgiven his very ashes, if by chance any of them are left. For whereas we are assured he designed his work for a complete body of all knowledge, human, divine, political, and mechanic, it is manifest he hath wholly neglected some, and been very imperfect perfect in the rest. For, first of all, as eminent a cabalist as his disciples would represent him, his account of the *opus magnum* is extremely poor and deficient; he seems to have read but very superficially either Sendivogus, Behmen, or Anthroposophia Theomagica. He is also quite mistaken about the *sphæra pyroplastica*, a neglect not to be atoned for, and (if the reader will admit so severe a censure) *vix crederem autorem hunc unquam audivisse ignis vocem*. His failings are not less prominent in several parts of the mechanics. For having read his writings with the utmost application usual among modern wits, I could never yet discover the least direction about the structure of that useful instrument a save-all; for want of which, if the moderns had not lent their assistance, we might yet have wandered in the dark. But I have still behind a fault far more notorious to tax this author with; I mean his gross ignorance in the common laws of this realm, and in the doctrine as well as discipline of the Church of England. A defect, indeed, for which both he and all the ancients stand most justly censured by my worthy and ingenious friend Mr. Wotton, Bachelor of Divinity, in his incomparable treatise of ancient and modern learning; a book never to be sufficiently valued, whether we consider the happy turns and flowings of the author's wit, the great usefulness of his sublime discoveries upon the subject of flies and spittle, or the laborious eloquence of his style. And I cannot forbear doing that author the justice of my public acknowledgments for the great helps and liftings I had out of his incomparable piece while I was penning this treatise.

But besides these omissions in Homer already mentioned, the curious reader will also observe several defects in that author's writings for which he is not altogether so accountable. For whereas every branch of knowledge has received such wonderful acquirements since his age, especially within these last three years or thereabouts, it is almost impossible he could be so very perfect in modern discoveries as his advocates pretend. We freely acknowledge him to be the inventor of the compass, of gunpowder, and the circulation of the blood; but I challenge any of his admirers to show me in all his writings a complete account of the spleen. Does he not also leave us wholly to seek in the art of political wagering? What can be more defective and unsatisfactory than his long dissertation upon tea? and as to his method of salivation without mercury, so much celebrated of late, it is to my own knowledge and experience a thing very little to be relied on.

It was to supply such momentous defects that I have been prevailed on, after long solicitation, to take pen in hand, and I dare venture to promise the judicious reader shall find nothing neglected here that can be of use upon any emergency of life. I am confident to have included and exhausted all that human imagination can rise or fall to. Particularly I recommend to the perusal of the learned certain discoveries that are wholly untouched by others, whereof I shall only mention, among a great many more, my "New Help of Smatterers, or the Art of being Deep Learned and Shallow Read," "A Curious Invention about Mouse-traps," "A Universal Rule of Reason, or Every Man his own Carver," together with a most useful engine for catching of owls. All which the judicious reader will find largely treated on in the several parts of this discourse.

I hold myself obliged to give as much light as possible into the beauties and excellences of what I am writing, because it is become the fashion and humour most applauded among the first authors of this polite and learned age, when they would correct the ill nature of critical or inform the ignorance of courteous readers. Besides, there have been several famous pieces lately published, both in verse and prose, wherein if the writers had not been pleased, out of their great humanity and affection to the public, to give us a nice detail of the sublime and the admirable they contain, it is a thousand to one whether we should ever have discovered one grain of either. For my own particular, I cannot deny that whatever I have said upon this occasion had been more proper in a preface, and more agreeable to the mode which usually directs it there. But I here think fit to lay hold on that great and honourable privilege of being the last writer. I claim an absolute authority in right as the freshest modern, which gives me a despotic power over all authors before me. In the strength of which title I do utterly disapprove and declare against that pernicious custom of making the preface a bill of fare to the book. For I have always looked upon it as a high point of indiscretion in monstermongers and other retailers of strange sights to hang out a fair large picture over the door, drawn after the life, with a most eloquent description underneath. This has saved me many a threepence, for my curiosity was fully satisfied, and I never offered to go in, though often invited by the urging and attending orator with his last moving and standing piece of rhetoric, "Sir, upon my word, we are just going to begin." Such is exactly the fate at this time of Prefaces, Epistles, Advertisements, Introductions, Prolegomenas, Apparatuses, To the Readers's. This expedient was admirable at first; our great Dryden has long carried it as far as it would go, and with incredible success. He has often said to me in confidence that the world would never have suspected him to be so great a poet if he had not assured them so frequently in his prefaces, that it was impossible they could either doubt or forget it. Perhaps it may be so. However, I much fear his instructions have edified out of their place, and taught men to grow wiser in certain points where he never intended they should; for it is lamentable to behold with what a lazy scorn many of the yawning readers in our age do now-a-days twirl over forty or fifty pages of preface and dedication (which is the usual modern stint), as if it were so much Latin. Though it must be also allowed, on the other hand, that a very considerable number is known to proceed critics and wits by reading nothing else. Into which two factions I think all present readers may justly be divided. Now, for myself, I profess to be of the former sort, and therefore having the modern inclination to expatiate upon the beauty of my own productions, and display the bright parts of my discourse, I thought best to do it in the body of the work, where as it now lies it makes a very considerable addition to the bulk of the volume, a circumstance by no means to be neglected by a skilful writer.

Having thus paid my due deference and acknowledgment to an established custom of our newest authors, by a long digression unsought for and a universal censure unprovoked, by forcing into the light, with much pains and dexterity, my own excellences and other men's defaults, with great justice to myself and candour to them, I now happily resume my subject, to the infinite satisfaction both of the reader and the author.

Section VI

A TALE OF A TUB

We left Lord Peter in open rupture with his two brethren, both for ever discarded from his house, and resigned to the wide world with little or nothing to trust to. Which are circumstances that render them proper subjects for the charity of a writer's pen to work on, scenes of misery ever affording the fairest harvest for great adventures. And in this the world may perceive the difference between the integrity of a generous Author and that of a common friend. The latter is observed to adhere close in prosperity, but on the decline of fortune to drop suddenly off; whereas the generous author, just on the contrary, finds his hero on the dunghill, from thence, by gradual steps, raises him to a throne, and then immediately withdraws, expecting not so much as thanks for his pains; in imitation of which example I have placed Lord Peter in a noble house, given him a title to wear and money to spend. There I shall leave him for some time, returning, where common charity directs me, to the assistance of his two brothers at their lowest ebb. However, I shall by no means forget my character of a historian, to follow the truth step by step whatever happens, or wherever it may lead me.

The two exiles so nearly united in fortune and interest took a lodging together, where at their first leisure they began to reflect on the numberless misfortunes and vexations of their life past, and could not tell of the sudden to what failure in their conduct they ought to impute them, when, after some recollection, they called to mind the copy of their father's will which they had so happily recovered. This was immediately produced, and a firm resolution taken between them to alter whatever was already amiss, and reduce all their future measures to the strictest obedience prescribed therein. The main body of the will (as the reader cannot easily have forgot) consisted in certain admirable rules, about the wearing of their coats, in the perusal whereof the two brothers at every period duly comparing the doctrine with the practice, there was never seen a wider difference between two things, horrible downright transgressions of every point. Upon which they both resolved without further delay to fall immediately upon reducing the whole exactly after their father's model.

But here it is good to stop the hasty reader, ever impatient to see the end of an adventure before we writers can duly prepare him for it. I am to record that these two brothers began to be distinguished at this time by certain names. One of them desired to be called Martin, and the other took the appellation of Jack. These two had lived in much friendship and agreement under the tyranny of their brother Peter, as it is the talent of fellow-sufferers to do, men in misfortune being like men in the dark, to whom all colours are the same. But when they came forward into the world, and began to display themselves to each other and to the light, their complexions appeared extremely different, which the present posture of their affairs gave them sudden opportunity to discover.

But here the severe reader may justly tax me as a writer of short memory, a deficiency to which a true modern cannot but of necessity be a little subject. Because, memory being an employment of the mind upon things past, is a faculty for which the learned in our illustrious age have no manner of occasion, who deal entirely with invention and strike all things out of themselves, or at least by collision from each other; upon which account, we think it highly reasonable to produce our great forgetfulness as an argument unanswerable for our great wit. I ought in method to have informed the reader about fifty pages ago of a fancy Lord Peter took, and infused into his brothers, to wear on their coats whatever trimmings came up in fashion, never pulling off any as they went out of the mode, but keeping on all together, which amounted in time to a medley the most antic you can possibly conceive, and this to a degree that, upon the time of their falling out, there was hardly a thread of the original coat to be seen, but an infinite quantity of lace, and ribbands, and fringe, and embroidery, and points (I mean only those tagged with silver, for the rest fell off). Now this material circumstance having been forgot in due place, as good fortune hath ordered, comes in very properly here, when the two brothers are just going to reform their vestures into the primitive state prescribed by their father's will.

They both unanimously entered upon this great work, looking sometimes on their coats and sometimes on the will. Martin laid the first hand; at one twitch brought off a large handful of points, and with a second pull stripped away ten dozen yards of fringe. But when he had gone thus far he demurred a while. He knew very well there yet remained a great deal more to be done; however, the first heat being over, his violence began to cool, and he resolved to proceed more moderately in the rest of the work, having already very narrowly escaped a swinging rent in pulling off the points, which being tagged with silver (as we have observed before), the judicious workman had with much sagacity double sewn to preserve them from falling. Resolving therefore to rid his coat of a huge quantity of gold lace, he picked up the stitches with much caution and diligently gleaned out all the loose threads as he went, which proved to be a work of time. Then he fell about the embroidered Indian figures of men, women, and children, against which, as you have heard in its due place, their father's testament was extremely exact and severe. These, with much dexterity and application, were after a while quite eradicated or utterly defaced. For the rest, where he observed the embroidery to be worked so close as not to be got away without damaging the cloth, or where it served to hide or strengthened any flaw in the body of the coat, contracted by the perpetual tampering of workmen upon it, he concluded the wisest course was to let it remain, resolving in no case whatsoever that the substance of the stuff should suffer injury, which he thought the best method for serving the true intent and meaning of his father's will. And this is the nearest account I have been able to collect of Martin's proceedings upon this great revolution.

But his brother Jack, whose adventures will be so extraordinary as to furnish a great part in the remainder of this discourse, entered upon the matter with other thoughts and a quite different spirit. For the memory of Lord Peter's injuries produced a degree of hatred and spite which had a much greater share of inciting him than any regards after his father's commands, since these appeared at best only secondary and subservient to the other. However, for this medley of humour he made a shift to find a very plausible name, honouring it with the title of zeal, which is, perhaps, the most significant word that has been ever yet produced in any language, as, I think, I have fully proved in my excellent analytical discourse upon that subject, wherein I have deduced a histori-theo-physiological account of zeal, showing how it first proceeded from a notion into a word, and from thence in a hot summer ripened into a tangible substance. This work, containing three large volumes in folio, I design very shortly to publish by the modern way of subscription, not doubting but the nobility and gentry of the land will give me all possible encouragement, having already had such a taste of what I am able to perform.

I record, therefore, that brother Jack, brimful of this miraculous compound, reflecting with indignation upon Peter's tyranny, and further provoked by the despondency of Martin, prefaced his resolutions to this purpose. "What!" said he, "a rogue that locked up his drink, turned away our wives, cheated us of our fortunes, palmed his crusts upon us for mutton, and at last kicked us out of doors; must we be in his fashions? A rascal, besides, that all the street cries out against." Having thus kindled and inflamed himself as high as possible, and by consequence in a delicate temper for beginning a reformation, he set about the work immediately, and in three minutes made more dispatch than Martin had done in as many hours. For, courteous reader, you are given to understand that zeal is never so highly obliged as when you set it a-tearing; and Jack, who doted on that quality in himself, allowed it at this time its full swing. Thus it happened that, stripping down a parcel of gold lace a little too hastily, he rent the main body of his coat from top to bottom; and whereas his talent was not of the happiest in taking up a stitch, he knew no better way than to darn it again with packthread thread and a skewer. But the matter was yet infinitely worse (I record it with tears) when he proceeded to the embroidery; for being clumsy of nature, and of temper impatient withal, beholding millions of stitches that required the nicest hand and sedatest constitution to extricate, in a great rage he tore off the whole piece, cloth and all, and flung it into the kennel, and furiously thus continuing his career, "Ah! good brother Martin," said he, "do as I do, for the love of God; strip, tear, pull, rend, flay off all that we may appear as unlike that rogue Peter as it is possible. I would not for a hundred pounds carry the least mark about me that might give occasion to the neighbours of suspecting I was related to such a rascal." But Martin, who at this time happened to be extremely phlegmatic and sedate, begged his brother, of all love, not to damage his coat by any means, for he never would get such another; desired him to consider that it was not their business to form their actions by any reflection upon Peter's, but by observing the rules prescribed in their father's will. That he should remember Peter was still their brother, whatever faults or injuries he had committed, and therefore they should by all means avoid such a thought as that of taking measures for good and evil from no other rule than of opposition to him. That it was true the testament of their good father was very exact in what related to the wearing of their coats; yet was it no less penal and strict in prescribing agreement, and friendship, and affection between them. And therefore, if straining a point were at all defensible, it would certainly be so rather to the advance of unity than increase of contradiction.

JONATHAN SWIFT

Martin had still proceeded as gravely as he began, and doubtless would have delivered an admirable lecture of morality, which might have exceedingly contributed to my reader's repose both of body and mind (the true ultimate end of ethics), but Jack was already gone a flight-shot beyond his patience. And as in scholastic disputes nothing serves to rouse the spleen of him that opposes so much as a kind of pedantic affected calmness in the respondent, disputants being for the most part like unequal scales, where the gravity of one side advances the lightness of the other, and causes it to fly up and kick the beam; so it happened here that the weight of Martin's arguments exalted Jack's levity, and made him fly out and spurn against his brother's moderation. In short, Martin's patience put Jack in a rage; but that which most afflicted him was to observe his brother's coat so well reduced into the state of innocence, while his own was either wholly rent to his shirt, or those places which had escaped his cruel clutches were still in Peter's livery. So that he looked like a drunken beau half rifled by bullies, or like a fresh tenant of Newgate when he has refused the payment of garnish, or like a discovered shoplifter left to the mercy of Exchange-women, or like a bawd in her old velvet petticoat resigned into the secular hands of the mobile. Like any or like all of these, a medley of rags, and lace, and fringes, unfortunate Jack did now appear; he would have been extremely glad to see his coat in the condition of Martin's, but infinitely gladder to find that of Martin in the same predicament with his. However, since neither of these was likely to come to pass, he thought fit to lend the whole business another turn, and to dress up necessity into a virtue. Therefore, after as many of the fox's arguments as he could muster up for bringing Martin to reason, as he called it, or as he meant it, into his own ragged, bobtailed condition, and observing he said all to little purpose, what alas! was left for the forlorn Jack to do, but, after a million of scurrilities against his brother, to run mad with spleen, and spite, and contradiction. To be short, here began a mortal breach between these two. Jack went immediately to new lodgings, and in a few days it was for certain reported that he had run out of his wits. In a short time after he appeared abroad, and confirmed the report by falling into the oddest whimsies that ever a sick brain conceived.

And now the little boys in the streets began to salute him with several names. Sometimes they would call him Jack the Bald, sometimes Jack with a Lanthorn, sometimes Dutch Jack, sometimes French Hugh, sometimes Tom the Beggar, and sometimes Knocking Jack of the North. And it was under one or some or all of these appellations (which I leave the learned reader to determine) that he hath given rise to the most illustrious and epidemic sect of Æolists, who, with honourable commemoration, do still acknowledge the renowned Jack for their author and founder. Of whose originals as well as principles I am now advancing to gratify the world with a very particular account.

"Mellæo contingens cuncta lepore."

Section VII

A Digression in Praise of Digressions

I have sometimes heard of an Iliad in a nut-shell, but it has been my fortune to have much oftener seen a nut-shell in an Iliad. There is no doubt that human life has received most wonderful advantages from both; but to which of the two the world is chiefly indebted, I shall leave among the curious as a problem worthy of their utmost inquiry. For the invention of the latter, I think the commonwealth of learning is chiefly obliged to the great modern improvement of digressions. The late refinements in knowledge, running parallel to those of diet in our nation, which among men of a judicious taste are dressed up in various compounds, consisting in soups and olios, fricassees and ragouts.

It is true there is a sort of morose, detracting, ill-bred people who pretend utterly to disrelish these polite innovations. And as to the similitude from diet, they allow the parallel, but are so bold as to pronounce the example itself a corruption and degeneracy of taste. They tell us that the fashion of jumbling fifty things together in a dish was at first introduced in compliance to a depraved and debauched appetite, as well as to a crazy constitution, and to see a man hunting through an olio after the head and brains of a goose, a widgeon, or a woodcock, is a sign he wants a stomach and digestion for more substantial victuals. Further, they affirm that digressions in a book are like foreign troops in a state, which argue the nation to want a heart and hands of its own, and often either subdue the natives, or drive them into the most unfruitful corners.

But after all that can be objected by these supercilious censors, it is manifest the society of writers would quickly be reduced to a very inconsiderable number if men were put upon making books with the fatal confinement of delivering nothing beyond what is to the purpose. It is acknowledged that were the case the same among us as with the Greeks and Romans, when learning was in its cradle, to be reared and fed and clothed by invention, it would be an easy task to fill up volumes upon particular occasions without further expatiating from the subject than by moderate excursions, helping to advance or clear the main design. But with knowledge it has fared as with a numerous army encamped in a fruitful country, which for a few days maintains itself by the product of the soil it is on, till provisions being spent, they send to forage many a mile among friends or enemies, it matters not. Meanwhile the neighbouring fields, trampled and beaten down, become barren and dry, affording no sustenance but clouds of dust.

The whole course of things being thus entirely changed between us and the ancients, and the moderns wisely sensible of it, we of this age have discovered a shorter and more prudent method to become scholars and wits, without the fatigue of reading or of thinking. The most accomplished way of using books at present is twofold: either first to serve them as some men do lords, learn their titles exactly, and then brag of their acquaintance; or, secondly, which is indeed the choicer, the profounder, and politer method, to get a thorough insight into the index by which the whole book is governed and turned, like fishes by the tail. For to enter the palace of learning at the great gate requires an expense of time and forms, therefore men of much haste and little ceremony are content to get in by the back-door. For the arts are all in a flying march, and therefore more easily subdued by attacking them in the rear. Thus physicians discover the state of the whole body by consulting only what comes from behind. Thus men catch knowledge by throwing their wit on the posteriors of a book, as boys do sparrows with flinging salt upon their tails. Thus human life is best understood by the wise man's rule of regarding the end. Thus are the sciences found, like Hercules' oxen, by tracing them backwards. Thus are old sciences unravelled like old stockings, by beginning at the foot.

Besides all this, the army of the sciences hath been of late with a world of martial discipline drawn into its close order, so that a view or a muster may be taken of it with abundance of expedition. For this great blessing we are wholly indebted to systems and abstracts, in which the modern fathers of learning, like prudent usurers, spent their sweat for the ease of us their children. For labour is the seed of idleness, and it is the peculiar happiness of our noble age to gather the fruit.

Now the method of growing wise, learned, and sublime having become so regular an affair, and so established in all its forms, the number of writers must needs have increased accordingly, and to a pitch that has made it of absolute necessity for them to interfere continually with each other. Besides, it is reckoned that there is not at this present a sufficient quantity of new matter left in Nature to furnish and adorn any one particular subject to the extent of a volume. This I am told by a very skilful computer, who hath given a full demonstration of it from rules of arithmetic.

This perhaps may be objected against by those who maintain the infinity of matter, and therefore will not allow that any species of it can be exhausted. For answer to which, let us examine the noblest branch of modern wit or invention planted and cultivated by the present age, and which of all others hath borne the most and the fairest fruit. For though some remains of it were left us by the ancients, yet have not any of those, as I remember, been translated or compiled into systems for modern use. Therefore we may affirm, to our own honour, that it has in some sort been both invented and brought to a perfection by the same hands. What I mean is, that highly celebrated talent among the modern wits of deducing similitudes, allusions, and applications, very surprising, agreeable, and apposite, from the signs of either sex, together with their proper uses. And truly, having observed how little invention bears any vogue besides what is derived into these channels, I have sometimes had a thought that the happy genius of our age and country was prophetically held forth by that ancient typical description of the Indian pigmies whose stature did not exceed above two feet, *sed quorum pudenda crassa, et ad talos usque pertingentia.* Now I have been very curious to inspect the late productions, wherein the beauties of this kind have most prominently appeared. And although this vein hath bled so freely, and all endeavours have been used in the power of human breath to dilate, extend, and keep it open, like the Scythians, who had a custom and an instrument to blow up those parts of their mares, that they might yield the more milk; yet I am under an apprehension it is near growing dry and past all recovery, and that either some new *fonde* of wit should, if possible, be provided, or else that we must e'en be content with repetition here as well as upon all other occasions.

This will stand as an uncontestable argument that our modern wits are not to reckon upon the infinity of matter for a constant supply. What remains, therefore, but that our last recourse must be had to large indexes and little compendiums? Quotations must be plentifully gathered and booked in alphabet. To this end, though authors need be little consulted, yet critics, and commentators, and lexicons carefully must. But above all, those judicious collectors of bright parts, and flowers, and observandas are to be nicely dwelt on by some called the sieves and boulters of learning, though it is left undetermined whether they dealt in pearls or meal, and consequently whether we are more to value that which passed through or what stayed behind.

By these methods, in a few weeks there starts up many a writer capable of managing the profoundest and most universal subjects. For what though his head be empty, provided his commonplace book be full? And if you will bate him but the circumstances of method, and style, and grammar, and invention; allow him but the common privileges of transcribing from others, and digressing from himself as often as he shall see occasion, he will desire no more ingredients towards fitting up a treatise that shall make a very comely figure on a bookseller's shelf, there to be preserved neat and clean for a long eternity, adorned with the heraldry of its title fairly inscribed on a label, never to be thumbed or greased by students, nor bound to everlasting chains of darkness in a library, but when the fulness of time is come shall happily undergo the trial of purgatory in order to ascend the sky.

Without these allowances how is it possible we modern wits should ever have an opportunity to introduce our collections listed under so many thousand heads of a different nature, for want of which the learned world would be deprived of infinite delight as well as instruction, and we ourselves buried beyond redress in an inglorious and undistinguished oblivion?

From such elements as these I am alive to behold the day wherein the corporation of authors can outvie all its brethren in the field—a happiness derived to us, with a great many others, from our Scythian ancestors, among whom the number of pens was so infinite that the Grecian eloquence had no other way of expressing it than by saying that in the regions far to the north it was hardly possible for a man to travel, the very air was so replete with feathers.

The necessity of this digression will easily excuse the length, and I have chosen for it as proper a place as I could readily find. If the judicious reader can assign a fitter, I do here empower him to remove it into any other corner he please. And so I return with great alacrity to pursue a more important concern.

Section VIII

A TALE OF A TUB

The learned Æolists maintain the original cause of all things to be wind, from which principle this whole universe was at first produced, and into which it must at last be resolved, that the same breath which had kindled and blew up the flame of Nature should one day blow it out.

"Quod procul à nobis flectat Fortuna gubernans."

This is what the Adepti understand by their *anima mundi*, that is to say, the spirit, or breath, or wind of the world; or examine the whole system by the particulars of Nature, and you will find it not to be disputed. For whether you please to call the *forma informans* of man by the name of *spiritus*, *animus*, *afflatus*, or *anima*, what are all these but several appellations for wind, which is the ruling element in every compound, and into which they all resolve upon their corruption. Further, what is life itself but, as it is commonly called, the breath of our nostrils, whence it is very justly observed by naturalists that wind still continues of great emolument in certain mysteries not to be named, giving occasion for those happy epithets of *turgidus* and *inflatus*, applied either to the emittent or recipient organs.

By what I have gathered out of ancient records, I find the compass of their doctrine took in two-and-thirty points, wherein it would be tedious to be very particular. However, a few of their most important precepts deducible from it are by no means to be omitted; among which, the following maxim was of much weight: That since wind had the master share as well as operation in every compound, by consequence those beings must be of chief excellence wherein that primordium appears most prominently to abound, and therefore man is in highest perfection of all created things, as having, by the great bounty of philosophers, been endued with three distinct *animas* or winds, to which the sage Æolists, with much liberality, have added a fourth, of equal necessity as well as ornament with the other three, by this *quartum principium* taking in the four corners of the world. Which gave occasion to that renowned cabalist Bombastus of placing the body of man in due position to the four cardinal points.

In consequence of this, their next principle was that man brings with him into the world a peculiar portion or grain of wind, which may be called a *quinta essentia* extracted from the other four. This quintessence is of catholic use upon all emergencies of life, is improveable into all arts and sciences, and may be wonderfully refined as well as enlarged by certain methods in education. This, when blown up to its perfection, ought not to be covetously boarded up, stifled, or hid under a bushel, but freely communicated to mankind. Upon these reasons, and others of equal weight, the wise Æolists affirm the gift of belching to be the noblest act of a rational creature. To cultivate which art, and render it more serviceable to mankind, they made use of several methods. At certain seasons of the year you might behold the priests amongst them in vast numbers with their mouths gaping wide against a storm. At other times were to be seen several hundreds linked together in a circular chain, with every man a pair of bellows applied to his neighbour, by which they blew up each other to the shape and size of a tun; and for that reason with great propriety of speech did usually call their bodies their vessels. When, by these and the like performances, they were grown sufficiently replete, they would immediately depart, and disembogue for the public good a plentiful share of their acquirements into their disciples' chaps. For we must here observe that all learning was esteemed among them to be compounded from the same principle. Because, first, it is generally affirmed or confessed that learning puffeth men up; and, secondly, they proved it by the following syllogism: "Words are but wind, and learning is nothing but words; ergo, learning is nothing but wind." For this reason the philosophers among them did in their schools deliver to their pupils all their doctrines and opinions by eructation, wherein they had acquired a wonderful eloquence, and of incredible variety. But the great characteristic by which their chief sages were best distinguished was a certain position of countenance, which gave undoubted intelligence to what degree or proportion the spirit agitated the inward mass. For after certain gripings, the wind and vapours issuing forth, having first by their turbulence and convulsions within caused an earthquake in man's little world, distorted the mouth, bloated the cheeks, and gave the eyes a terrible kind of relievo. At which junctures all their belches were received for sacred, the sourer the better, and swallowed with infinite consolation by their meagre devotees. And to render these yet more complete, because the breath of man's life is in his nostrils, therefore the choicest, most edifying, and most enlivening belches were very wisely conveyed through that vehicle to give them a tincture as they passed.

Their gods were the four winds, whom they worshipped as the spirits that pervade and enliven the universe, and as those from whom alone all inspiration can properly be said to proceed. However, the chief of these, to whom they performed the adoration of Latria, was the Almighty North, an ancient deity, whom the inhabitants of Megalopolis in Greece had likewise in highest reverence. "Omnium deorum Boream maxime celebrant." This god, though endued with ubiquity, was yet supposed by the profounder Æolists to possess one peculiar habitation, or (to speak in form) a *cælum empyræum*, wherein he was more intimately present. This was situated in a certain region well known to the ancient Greeks, by them called Σχοτία, the Land of Darkness. And although many controversies have arisen upon that matter, yet so much is undisputed, that from a region of the like denomination the most refined Æolists have borrowed their original, from whence in every age the zealous among their priesthood have brought over their choicest inspiration, fetching it with their own hands from the fountain-head in certain bladders, and disploding it among the sectaries in all nations, who did, and do, and ever will, daily gasp and pant after it.

Now their mysteries and rites were performed in this manner. It is well known among the learned that the virtuosos of former ages had a contrivance for carrying and preserving winds in casks or barrels, which was of great assistance upon long sea-voyages, and the loss of so useful an art at present is very much to be lamented, though, I know not how, with great negligence omitted by Pancirollus. It was an invention ascribed to Æolus himself, from whom this sect is denominated, and who, in honour of their founder's memory, have to this day preserved great numbers of those barrels, whereof they fix one in each of their temples, first beating out the top. Into this barrel upon solemn days the priest enters, where, having before duly prepared himself by the methods already described, a secret funnel is also conveyed to the bottom of the barrel, which admits new supplies of inspiration from a northern chink or cranny. Whereupon you behold him swell immediately to the shape and size of his vessel. In this posture he disembogues whole tempests upon his auditory, as the spirit from beneath gives him utterance, which issuing *ex adytis* and *penetralibus*, is not performed without much pain and griping. And the wind in breaking forth deals with his face as it does with that of the sea, first blackening, then wrinkling, and at last bursting it into a foam. It is in this guise the sacred Æolist delivers his oracular belches to his panting disciples, of whom some are greedily gaping after the sanctified breath, others are all the while hymning out the praises of the winds, and gently wafted to and fro by their own humming, do thus represent the soft breezes of their deities appeased.

It is from this custom of the priests that some authors maintain these Æolists to have been very ancient in the world, because the delivery of their mysteries, which I have just now mentioned, appears exactly the same with that of other ancient oracles, whose inspirations were owing to certain subterraneous effluviums of wind delivered with the same pain to the priest, and much about the same influence on the people. It is true indeed that these were frequently managed and directed by female officers, whose organs were understood to be better disposed for the admission of those oracular gusts, as entering and passing up through a receptacle of greater capacity, and causing also a pruriency by the way, such as with due management has been refined from carnal into a spiritual ecstasy. And to strengthen this profound conjecture, it is further insisted that this custom of female priests is kept up still in certain refined colleges of our modern Æolists, who are agreed to receive their inspiration, derived through the receptacle aforesaid, like their ancestors the Sybils.

And whereas the mind of man, when he gives the spur and bridle to his thoughts, does never stop, but naturally sallies out into both extremes of high and low, of good and evil, his first flight of fancy commonly transports him to ideas of what is most perfect, finished, and exalted, till, having soared out of his own reach and sight, not well perceiving how near the frontiers of height and depth border upon each other, with the same course and wing he falls down plump into the lowest bottom of things, like one who travels the east into the west, or like a straight line drawn by its own length into a circle. Whether a tincture of malice in our natures makes us fond of furnishing every bright idea with its reverse, or whether reason, reflecting upon the sum of things, can, like the sun, serve only to enlighten one half of the globe, leaving the other half by necessity under shade and darkness, or whether fancy, flying up to the imagination of what is highest and best, becomes over-short, and spent, and weary, and suddenly falls, like a dead bird of paradise, to the ground; or whether, after all these metaphysical conjectures, I have not entirely missed the true reason; the proposition, however, which has stood me in so much circumstance is altogether true, that as the most uncivilised parts of mankind have some way or other climbed up into the conception of a God or Supreme Power, so they have seldom forgot to provide their fears with certain ghastly notions, which, instead of better, have served them pretty tolerably for a devil. And this proceeding seems to be natural enough, for it is with men whose imaginations are lifted up very high after the same rate as with those whose bodies are so, that as they are delighted with the advantage of a nearer contemplation upwards, so they are equally terrified with the dismal prospect of the precipice below. Thus in the choice of a devil it has been the usual method of mankind to single out some being, either in act or in vision, which was in most antipathy to the god they had framed. Thus also the sect of the Æolists possessed themselves with a dread and horror and hatred of two malignant natures, betwixt whom and the deities they adored perpetual enmity was established. The first of these was the chameleon, sworn foe to inspiration, who in scorn devoured large influences of their god, without refunding the smallest blast by eructation. The other was a huge terrible monster called Moulinavent, who with four strong arms waged eternal battle with all their divinities, dexterously turning to avoid their blows and repay them with interest.

Thus furnished, and set out with gods as well as devils, was the renowned sect of Æolists, which makes at this day so illustrious a figure in the world, and whereof that polite nation of Laplanders are beyond all doubt a most authentic branch, of whom I therefore cannot without injustice here omit to make honourable mention, since they appear to be so closely allied in point of interest as well as inclinations with their brother Æolists among us, as not only to buy their winds by wholesale from the same merchants, but also to retail them after the same rate and method, and to customers much alike.

Now whether the system here delivered was wholly compiled by Jack, or, as some writers believe, rather copied from the original at Delphos, with certain additions and emendations suited to times and circumstances, I shall not absolutely determine. This I may affirm, that Jack gave it at least a new turn, and formed it into the same dress and model as it lies deduced by me.

I have long sought after this opportunity of doing justice to a society of men for whom I have a peculiar honour, and whose opinions as well as practices have been extremely misrepresented and traduced by the malice or ignorance of their adversaries. For I think it one of the greatest and best of human actions to remove prejudices and place things in their truest and fairest light, which I therefore boldly undertake, without any regards of my own beside the conscience, the honour, and the thanks.

Section IX

A Digression Concerning the Original, the Use, and Improvement of Madness in a Commonwealth

Nor shall it any ways detract from the just reputation of this famous sect that its rise and institution are owing to such an author as I have described Jack to be, a person whose intellectuals were overturned and his brain shaken out of its natural position, which we commonly suppose to be a distemper, and call by the name of madness or frenzy. For if we take a survey of the greatest actions that have been performed in the world under the influence of single men, which are the establishment of new empires by conquest, the advance and progress of new schemes in philosophy, and the contriving as well as the propagating of new religions, we shall find the authors of them all to have been persons whose natural reason hath admitted great revolutions from their diet, their education, the prevalency of some certain temper, together with the particular influence of air and climate. Besides, there is something individual in human minds that easily kindles at the accidental approach and collision of certain circumstances, which, though of paltry and mean appearance, do often flame out into the greatest emergencies of life. For great turns are not always given by strong hands, but by lucky adaptation and at proper seasons, and it is of no import where the fire was kindled if the vapour has once got up into the brain. For the upper region of man is furnished like the middle region of the air, the materials are formed from causes of the widest difference, yet produce at last the same substance and effect. Mists arise from the earth, steams from dunghills, exhalations from the sea, and smoke from fire; yet all clouds are the same in composition as well as consequences, and the fumes issuing from a jakes will furnish as comely and useful a vapour as incense from an altar. Thus far, I suppose, will easily be granted me; and then it will follow that as the face of Nature never produces rain but when it is overcast and disturbed, so human understanding seated in the brain must be troubled and overspread by vapours ascending from the lower faculties to water the invention and render it fruitful. Now although these vapours (as it hath been already said) are of as various original as those of the skies, yet the crop they produce differs both in kind and degree, merely according to the soil. I will produce two instances to prove and explain what I am now advancing.

A certain great prince raised a mighty army, filled his coffers with infinite treasures, provided an invincible fleet, and all this without giving the least part of his design to his greatest ministers or his nearest favourites. Immediately the whole world was alarmed, the neighbouring crowns in trembling expectation towards what point the storm would burst, the small politicians everywhere forming profound conjectures. Some believed he had laid a scheme for universal monarchy; others, after much insight, determined the matter to be a project for pulling down the Pope and setting up the Reformed religion, which had once been his own. Some again, of a deeper sagacity, sent him into Asia to subdue the Turk and recover Palestine. In the midst of all these projects and preparations, a certain state-surgeon, gathering the nature of the disease by these symptoms, attempted the cure, at one blow performed the operation, broke the bag and out flew the vapour; nor did anything want to render it a complete remedy, only that the prince unfortunately happened to die in the performance. Now is the reader exceeding curious to learn from whence this vapour took its rise, which had so long set the nations at a gaze? What secret wheel, what hidden spring, could put into motion so wonderful an engine? It was afterwards discovered that the movement of this whole machine had been directed by an absent female, who was removed into an enemy's country. What should an unhappy prince do in such ticklish circumstances as these? He tried in vain the poet's never-failing receipt of *corpora quæque*, for

> *"Idque petit corpus mens unde est saucia amore;*
> *Unde feritur, eo tendit, gestitque coire."*
>
> —*Lucr*

Having to no purpose used all peaceable endeavours, the collected part of the semen, raised and inflamed, became adust, converted to choler, turned head upon the spinal duct, and ascended to the brain. The very same principle that influences a bully to break the windows of a woman who has jilted him naturally stirs up a great prince to raise mighty armies and dream of nothing but sieges, battles, and victories.

The other instance is what I have read somewhere in a very ancient author of a mighty king, who, for the space of above thirty years, amused himself to take and lose towns, beat armies and be beaten, drive princes out of their dominions, fright children from their bread and butter, burn, lay waste, plunder, dragoon, massacre subject and stranger, friend and foe, male and female. It is recorded that the philosophers of each country were in grave dispute upon causes natural, moral, and political, to find out where they should assign an original solution of this phenomenon. At last the vapour or spirit which animated the hero's brain, being in perpetual circulation, seized upon that region of the human body so renowned for furnishing the *zibeta occidentalis*, and gathering there into a tumour, left the rest of the world for that time in peace. Of such mighty consequence is it where those exhalations fix, and of so little from whence they proceed. The same spirits which in their superior progress would conquer a kingdom descending upon the anus, conclude in a fistula.

Let us next examine the great introducers of new schemes in philosophy, and search till we can find from what faculty of the soul the disposition arises in mortal man of taking it into his head to advance new systems with such an eager zeal in things agreed on all hands impossible to be known; from what seeds this disposition springs, and to what quality of human nature these grand innovators have been indebted for their number of disciples, because it is plain that several of the chief among them, both ancient and modern, were usually mistaken by their adversaries, and, indeed, by all, except their own followers, to have been persons crazed or out of their wits, having generally proceeded in the common course of their words and actions by a method very different from the vulgar dictates of unrefined reason, agreeing for the most part in their several models with their present undoubted successors in the academy of modern Bedlam, whose merits and principles I shall further examine in due place. Of this kind were Epicurus, Diogenes, Apollonius, Lucretius, Paracelsus, Des Cartes, and others, who, if they were now in the world, tied fast and separate from their followers, would in this our undistinguishing age incur manifest danger of phlebotomy, and whips, and chains, and dark chambers, and straw. For what man in the natural state or course of thinking did ever conceive it in his power to reduce the notions of all mankind exactly to the same length, and breadth, and height of his own? Yet this is the first humble and civil design of all innovators in the empire of reason. Epicurus modestly hoped that one time or other a certain fortuitous concourse of all men's opinions, after perpetual jostlings, the sharp with the smooth, the light and the heavy, the round and the square, would, by certain clinamina, unite in the notions of atoms and void, as these did in the originals of all things. Cartesius reckoned to see before he died the sentiments of all philosophers, like so many lesser stars in his romantic system, rapt and drawn within his own vortex. Now I would gladly be informed how it is possible to account for such imaginations as these in particular men, without recourse to my phenomenon of vapours ascending from the lower faculties to overshadow the brain, and there distilling into conceptions, for which the narrowness of our mother-tongue has not yet assigned any other name beside that of madness or frenzy. Let us therefore now conjecture how it comes to pass that none of these great prescribers do ever fail providing themselves and their notions with a number of implicit disciples, and I think the reason is easy to be assigned, for there is a peculiar string in the harmony of human understanding, which in several individuals is exactly of the same tuning. This, if you can dexterously screw up to its right key, and then strike gently upon it whenever you have the good fortune to light among those of the same pitch, they will by a secret necessary sympathy strike exactly at the same time. And in this one circumstance lies all the skill or luck of the matter; for, if you chance to jar the string among those who are either above or below your own height, instead of subscribing to your doctrine, they will tie you fast, call you mad, and feed you with bread and water. It is therefore a point of the nicest conduct to distinguish and adapt this noble talent with respect to the differences of persons and of times. Cicero understood this very well, when, writing to a friend in England, with a caution, among other matters, to beware of being cheated by our hackney-coachmen (who, it seems, in those days were as arrant rascals as they are now), has these remarkable words, *Est quod gaudeas te in ista loca venisse, ubi aliquid sapere viderere*. For, to speak a bold truth, it is a fatal miscarriage so ill to order affairs as to pass for a fool in one company, when in another you might be treated as a philosopher; which I desire some certain gentlemen of my acquaintance to lay up in their hearts as a very seasonable innuendo.

This, indeed, was the fatal mistake of that worthy gentleman, my most ingenious friend Mr. Wotton, a person in appearance ordained for great designs as well as performances, whether you will consider his notions or his looks. Surely no man ever advanced into the public with fitter qualifications of body and mind for the propagation of a new religion. Oh, had those happy talents, misapplied to vain philosophy, been turned into their proper channels of dreams and visions, where distortion of mind and countenance are of such sovereign use, the base, detracting world would not then have dared to report that something is amiss, that his brain hath undergone an unlucky shake, which even his brother modernists themselves, like ungrates, do whisper so loud that it reaches up to the very garret I am now writing in.

Lastly, whoever pleases to look into the fountains of enthusiasm, from whence in all ages have eternally proceeded such fattening streams, will find the spring-head to have been as troubled and muddy as the current. Of such great emolument is a tincture of this vapour, which the world calls madness, that without its help the world would not only be deprived of those two great blessings, conquests and systems, but even all mankind would unhappily be reduced to the same belief in things invisible. Now the former postulatum being held, that it is of no import from what originals this vapour proceeds, but either in what angles it strikes and spreads over the understanding, or upon what species of brain it ascends, it will be a very delicate point to cut the feather and divide the several reasons to a nice and curious reader, how this numerical difference in the brain can produce effects of so vast a difference from the same vapour as to be the sole point of individuation between Alexander the Great, Jack of Leyden, and Monsieur Des Cartes. The present argument is the most abstracted that ever I engaged in; it strains my faculties to their highest stretch, and I desire the reader to attend with utmost perpensity, for I now proceed to unravel this knotty point.

There is in mankind a certain. . . *Hic multa. . . desiderantur*. . . and this I take to be a clear solution of the matter.

Having, therefore, so narrowly passed through this intricate difficulty, the reader will, I am sure, agree with me in the conclusion that, if the moderns mean by madness only a disturbance or transposition of the brain, by force of certain vapours issuing up from the lower faculties, then has this madness been the parent of all those mighty revolutions that have happened in empire, in philosophy, and in religion. For the brain in its natural position and state of serenity disposeth its owner to pass his life in the common forms, without any thought of subduing multitudes to his own power, his reasons, or his visions, and the more he shapes his understanding by the pattern of human learning, the less he is inclined to form parties after his particular notions, because that instructs him in his private infirmities, as well as in the stubborn ignorance of the people. But when a man's fancy gets astride on his reason, when imagination is at cuffs with the senses, and common understanding as well as common sense is kicked out of doors, the first proselyte he makes is himself; and when that is once compassed, the difficulty is not so great in bringing over others, a strong delusion always operating from without as vigorously as from within. For cant and vision are to the ear and the eye the same that tickling is to the touch. Those entertainments and pleasures we most value in life are such as dupe and play the wag with the senses. For if we take an examination of what is generally understood by happiness, as it has respect either to the understanding or the senses we shall find all its properties and adjuncts will herd under this short definition, that it is a perpetual possession of being well deceived. And first, with relation to the mind or understanding, it is manifest what mighty advantages fiction has over truth, and the reason is just at our elbow: because imagination can build nobler scenes and produce more wonderful revolutions than fortune or Nature will be at the expense to furnish. Nor is mankind so much to blame in his choice thus determining him, if we consider that the debate merely lies between things past and things conceived, and so the question is only this: whether things that have place in the imagination may not as properly be said to exist as those that are seated in the memory? which may be justly held in the affirmative, and very much to the advantage of the former, since this is acknowledged to be the womb of things, and the other allowed to be no more than the grave. Again, if we take this definition of happiness and examine it with reference to the senses, it will be acknowledged wonderfully adapt. How sad and insipid do all objects accost us that are not conveyed in the vehicle of delusion! How shrunk is everything as it appears in the glass of Nature, so that if it were not for the assistance of artificial mediums, false lights, refracted angles, varnish, and tinsel, there would be a mighty level in the felicity and enjoyments of mortal men. If this were seriously considered by the world, as I have a certain reason to suspect it hardly will, men would no longer reckon among their high points of wisdom the art of exposing weak sides and publishing infirmities—an employment, in my opinion, neither better nor worse than that of unmasking, which, I think, has never been allowed fair usage, either in the world or the playhouse.

In the proportion that credulity is a more peaceful possession of the mind than curiosity, so far preferable is that wisdom which converses about the surface to that pretended philosophy which enters into the depths of things and then comes gravely back with informations and discoveries, that in the inside they are good for nothing. The two senses to which all objects first address themselves are the sight and the touch; these never examine farther than the colour, the shape, the size, and whatever other qualities dwell or are drawn by art upon the outward of bodies; and then comes reason officiously, with tools for cutting, and opening, and mangling, and piercing, offering to demonstrate that they are not of the same consistence quite through. Now I take all this to be the last degree of perverting Nature, one of whose eternal laws it is to put her best furniture forward. And therefore, in order to save the charges of all such expensive anatomy for the time to come, I do here think fit to inform the reader that in such conclusions as these reason is certainly in the right; and that in most corporeal beings which have fallen under my cognisance, the outside hath been infinitely preferable to the in, whereof I have been further convinced from some late experiments. Last week I saw a woman flayed, and you will hardly believe how much it altered her person for the worse. Yesterday I ordered the carcass of a beau to be stripped in my presence, when we were all amazed to find so many unsuspected faults under one suit of clothes. Then I laid open his brain, his heart, and his spleen, but I plainly perceived at every operation that the farther we proceeded, we found the defects increase upon us, in number and bulk; from all which I justly formed this conclusion to myself, that whatever philosopher or projector can find out an art to sodder and patch up the flaws and imperfections of Nature, will deserve much better of mankind and teach us a more useful science than that so much in present esteem, of widening and exposing them (like him who held anatomy to be the ultimate end of physic). And he whose fortunes and dispositions have placed him in a convenient station to enjoy the fruits of this noble art, he that can with Epicurus content his ideas with the films and images that fly off upon his senses from the superfices of things, such a man, truly wise, creams off Nature, leaving the sour and the dregs for philosophy and reason to lap up. This is the sublime and refined point of felicity called the possession of being well-deceived, the serene peaceful state of being a fool among knaves.

But to return to madness. It is certain that, according to the system I have above deduced, every species thereof proceeds from a redundancy of vapour; therefore, as some kinds of frenzy give double strength to the sinews, so there are of other species which add vigour, and life, and spirit to the brain. Now it usually happens that these active spirits, getting possession of the brain, resemble those that haunt other waste and empty dwellings, which for want of business either vanish and carry away a piece of the house, or else stay at home and fling it all out of the windows. By which are mystically displayed the two principal branches of madness, and which some philosophers, not considering so well as I, have mistook to be different in their causes, over-hastily assigning the first to deficiency and the other to redundance.

I think it therefore manifest, from what I have here advanced, that the main point of skill and address is to furnish employment for this redundancy of vapour, and prudently to adjust the seasons of it, by which means it may certainly become of cardinal and catholic emolument in a commonwealth. Thus one man, choosing a proper juncture, leaps into a gulf, from thence proceeds a hero, and is called the saviour of his country. Another achieves the same enterprise, but unluckily timing it, has left the brand of madness fixed as a reproach upon his memory. Upon so nice a distinction are we taught to repeat the name of Curtius with reverence and love, that of Empedocles with hatred and contempt. Thus also it is usually conceived that the elder Brutus only personated the fool and madman for the good of the public; but this was nothing else than a redundancy of the same vapour long misapplied, called by the Latins *ingenium par negotiis*, or (to translate it as nearly as I can), a sort of frenzy never in its right element till you take it up in business of the state.

Upon all which, and many other reasons of equal weight, though not equally curious, I do here gladly embrace an opportunity I have long sought for, of recommending it as a very noble undertaking to Sir Edward Seymour, Sir Christopher Musgrave, Sir John Bowles, John Howe, Esq., and other patriots concerned, that they would move for leave to bring in a Bill for appointing commissioners to inspect into Bedlam and the parts adjacent, who shall be empowered to send for persons, papers, and records, to examine into the merits and qualifications of every student and professor, to observe with utmost exactness their several dispositions and behaviour, by which means, duly distinguishing and adapting their talents, they might produce admirable instruments for the several offices in a state, . . . civil and military, proceeding in such methods as I shall here humbly propose. And I hope the gentle reader will give some allowance to my great solicitudes in this important affair, upon account of that high esteem I have ever borne that honourable society, whereof I had some time the happiness to be an unworthy member.

JONATHAN SWIFT

Is any student tearing his straw in piecemeal, swearing and blaspheming, biting his grate, foaming at the mouth, and emptying his vessel in the spectators' faces? Let the right worshipful the Commissioners of Inspection give him a regiment of dragoons, and send him into Flanders among the rest. Is another eternally talking, sputtering, gaping, bawling, in a sound without period or article? What wonderful talents are here mislaid! Let him be furnished immediately with a green bag and papers, and threepence in his pocket, and away with him to Westminster Hall. You will find a third gravely taking the dimensions of his kennel, a person of foresight and insight, though kept quite in the dark; for why, like Moses, *Ecce cornuta erat ejus facies*. He walks duly in one pace, entreats your penny with due gravity and ceremony, talks much of hard times, and taxes, and the whore of Babylon, bars up the wooden of his cell constantly at eight o'clock, dreams of fire, and shoplifters, and court-customers, and privileged places. Now what a figure would all these acquirements amount to if the owner were sent into the City among his brethren! Behold a fourth in much and deep conversation with himself, biting his thumbs at proper junctures, his countenance chequered with business and design; sometimes walking very fast, with his eyes nailed to a paper that he holds in his hands; a great saver of time, somewhat thick of hearing, very short of sight, but more of memory; a man ever in haste, a great hatcher and breeder of business, and excellent at the famous art of whispering nothing; a huge idolator of monosyllables and procrastination, so ready to give his word to everybody that he never keeps it; one that has forgot the common meaning of words, but an admirable retainer of the sound; extremely subject to the looseness, for his occasions are perpetually calling him away. If you approach his grate in his familiar intervals, "Sir," says he, "give me a penny and I'll sing you a song; but give me the penny first" (hence comes the common saying and commoner practice of parting with money for a song). What a complete system of court-skill is here described in every branch of it, and all utterly lost with wrong application! Accost the hole of another kennel, first stopping your nose, you will behold a surly, gloomy, nasty, slovenly mortal, raking in his own dung and dabbling in his urine. The best part of his diet is the reversion of his own ordure, which expiring into steams, whirls perpetually about, and at last reinfunds. His complexion is of a dirty yellow, with a thin scattered beard, exactly agreeable to that of his diet upon its first declination, like other insects, who, having their birth and education in an excrement, from thence borrow their colour and their smell. The student of this apartment is very sparing of his words, but somewhat over-liberal of his breath. He holds his hand out ready to receive your penny, and immediately upon receipt withdraws to his former occupations. Now is it not amazing to think the society of Warwick Lane should have no more concern for the recovery of so useful a member, who, if one may judge from these appearances, would become the greatest ornament to that illustrious body? Another student struts up fiercely to your teeth, puffing with his lips, half squeezing out his eyes, and very graciously holds out his hand to kiss. The keeper desires you not to be afraid of this professor, for he will do you no hurt; to him alone is allowed the liberty of the ante-chamber, and the orator of the place gives you to understand that this solemn person is a tailor run mad with pride. This considerable student is adorned with many other qualities, upon which at present I shall not further enlarge. . . Hark in your ear. . . I am strangely mistaken if all his address, his motions, and his airs would not then be very natural and in their proper element.

I shall not descend so minutely as to insist upon the vast number of beaux, fiddlers, poets, and politicians that the world might recover by such a reformation, but what is more material, beside the clear gain redounding to the commonwealth by so large an acquisition of persons to employ, whose talents and acquirements, if I may be so bold to affirm it, are now buried or at least misapplied. It would be a mighty advantage accruing to the public from this inquiry that all these would very much excel and arrive at great perfection in their several kinds, which I think is manifest from what I have already shown, and shall enforce by this one plain instance, that even I myself, the author of these momentous truths, am a person whose imaginations are hard-mouthed and exceedingly disposed to run away with his reason, which I have observed from long experience to be a very light rider, and easily shook off; upon which account my friends will never trust me alone without a solemn promise to vent my speculations in this or the like manner, for the universal benefit of human kind, which perhaps the gentle, courteous, and candid reader, brimful of that modern charity and tenderness usually annexed to his office, will be very hardly persuaded to believe.

Section X

A Farther Digression

It is an unanswerable argument of a very refined age the wonderful civilities that have passed of late years between the nation of authors and that of readers. There can hardly pop out a play, a pamphlet, or a poem without a preface full of acknowledgments to the world for the general reception and applause they have given it, which the Lord knows where, or when, or how, or from whom it received. In due deference to so laudable a custom, I do here return my humble thanks to His Majesty and both Houses of Parliament, to the Lords of the King's most honourable Privy Council, to the reverend the Judges, to the Clergy, and Gentry, and Yeomanry of this land; but in a more especial manner to my worthy brethren and friends at Will's Coffee-house, and Gresham College, and Warwick Lane, and Moorfields, and Scotland Yard, and Westminster Hall, and Guildhall; in short, to all inhabitants and retainers whatsoever, either in court, or church, or camp, or city, or country, for their generosity and universal acceptance of this divine treatise. I accept their approbation and good opinion with extreme gratitude, and to the utmost of my poor capacity shall take hold of all opportunities to return the obligation.

I am also happy that fate has flung me into so blessed an age for the mutual felicity of booksellers and authors, whom I may safely affirm to be at this day the two only satisfied parties in England. Ask an author how his last piece has succeeded, "Why, truly he thanks his stars the world has been very favourable, and he has not the least reason to complain." And yet he wrote it in a week at bits and starts, when he could steal an hour from his urgent affairs, as it is a hundred to one you may see further in the preface, to which he refers you, and for the rest to the bookseller. There you go as a customer, and make the same question, "He blesses his God the thing takes wonderful; he is just printing a second edition, and has but three left in his shop." "You beat down the price; sir, we shall not differ," and in hopes of your custom another time, lets you have it as reasonable as you please; "And pray send as many of your acquaintance as you will; I shall upon your account furnish them all at the same rate."

Now it is not well enough considered to what accidents and occasions the world is indebted for the greatest part of those noble writings which hourly start up to entertain it. If it were not for a rainy day, a drunken vigil, a fit of the spleen, a course of physic, a sleepy Sunday, an ill run at dice, a long tailor's bill, a beggar's purse, a factious head, a hot sun, costive diet, want of books, and a just contempt of learning,—but for these events, I say, and some others too long to recite (especially a prudent neglect of taking brimstone inwardly), I doubt the number of authors and of writings would dwindle away to a degree most woeful to behold. To confirm this opinion, hear the words of the famous troglodyte philosopher. "It is certain," said he, "some grains of folly are of course annexed as part in the composition of human nature; only the choice is left us whether we please to wear them inlaid or embossed, and we need not go very far to seek how that is usually determined, when we remember it is with human faculties as with liquors, the lightest will be ever at the top."

There is in this famous island of Britain a certain paltry scribbler, very voluminous, whose character the reader cannot wholly be a stranger to. He deals in a pernicious kind of writings called "Second Parts," and usually passes under the name of "The Author of the First." I easily foresee that as soon as I lay down my pen this nimble operator will have stole it, and treat me as inhumanly as he has already done Dr. Blackmore, Lestrange, and many others who shall here be nameless. I therefore fly for justice and relief into the hands of that great rectifier of saddles and lover of mankind, Dr. Bentley, begging he will take this enormous grievance into his most modern consideration; and if it should so happen that the furniture of an ass in the shape of a second part must for my sins be clapped, by mistake, upon my back, that he will immediately please, in the presence of the world, to lighten me of the burthen, and take it home to his own house till the true beast thinks fit to call for it.

In the meantime, I do here give this public notice that my resolutions are to circumscribe within this discourse the whole stock of matter I have been so many years providing. Since my vein is once opened, I am content to exhaust it all at a running, for the peculiar advantage of my dear country, and for the universal benefit of mankind. Therefore, hospitably considering the number of my guests, they shall have my whole entertainment at a meal, and I scorn to set up the leavings in the cupboard. What the guests cannot eat may be given to the poor, and the dogs under the table may gnaw the bones. This I understand for a more generous proceeding than to turn the company's stomachs by inviting them again to-morrow to a scurvy meal of scraps.

If the reader fairly considers the strength of what I have advanced in the foregoing section, I am convinced it will produce a wonderful revolution in his notions and opinions, and he will be abundantly better prepared to receive and to relish the concluding part of this miraculous treatise. Readers may be divided into three classes—the superficial, the ignorant, and the learned, and I have with much felicity fitted my pen to the genius and advantage of each. The superficial reader will be strangely provoked to laughter, which clears the breast and the lungs, is sovereign against the spleen, and the most innocent of all diuretics. The ignorant reader (between whom and the former the distinction is extremely nice) will find himself disposed to stare, which is an admirable remedy for ill eyes, serves to raise and enliven the spirits, and wonderfully helps perspiration. But the reader truly learned, chiefly for whose benefit I wake when others sleep, and sleep when others wake, will here find sufficient matter to employ his speculations for the rest of his life. It were much to be wished, and I do here humbly propose for an experiment, that every prince in Christendom will take seven of the deepest scholars in his dominions and shut them up close for seven years in seven chambers, with a command to write seven ample commentaries on this comprehensive discourse. I shall venture to affirm that, whatever difference may be found in their several conjectures, they will be all, without the least distortion, manifestly deducible from the text. Meantime it is my earnest request that so useful an undertaking may be entered upon (if their Majesties please) with all convenient speed, because I have a strong inclination before I leave the world to taste a blessing which we mysterious writers can seldom reach till we have got into our graves, whether it is that fame being a fruit grafted on the body, can hardly grow and much less ripen till the stock is in the earth, or whether she be a bird of prey, and is lured among the rest to pursue after the scent of a carcass, or whether she conceives her trumpet sounds best and farthest when she stands on a tomb, by the advantage of a rising ground and the echo of a hollow vault.

It is true, indeed, the republic of dark authors, after they once found out this excellent expedient of dying, have been peculiarly happy in the variety as well as extent of their reputation. For night being the universal mother of things, wise philosophers hold all writings to be fruitful in the proportion they are dark, and therefore the true illuminated (that is to say, the darkest of all) have met with such numberless commentators, whose scholiastic midwifery hath delivered them of meanings that the authors themselves perhaps never conceived, and yet may very justly be allowed the lawful parents of them, the words of such writers being like seed, which, however scattered at random, when they light upon a fruitful ground, will multiply far beyond either the hopes or imagination of the sower.

And therefore, in order to promote so useful a work, I will here take leave to glance a few innuendos that may be of great assistance to those sublime spirits who shall be appointed to labour in a universal comment upon this wonderful discourse. And first, I have couched a very profound mystery in the number of 0's multiplied by seven and divided by nine. Also, if a devout brother of the Rosy Cross will pray fervently for sixty-three mornings with a lively faith, and then transpose certain letters and syllables according to prescription, in the second and fifth section they will certainly reveal into a full receipt of the *opus magnum*. Lastly, whoever will be at the pains to calculate the whole number of each letter in this treatise, and sum up the difference exactly between the several numbers, assigning the true natural cause for every such difference, the discoveries in the product will plentifully reward his labour. But then he must beware of Bythus and Sigè, and be sure not to forget the qualities of Acamoth; *a cujus lacrymis humecta prodit substantia, à risu lucida, à tristitiâ solida, et à timore mobilis*, wherein Eugenius Philalethes hath committed an unpardonable mistake.

Section XI

A Tale of a Tub

After so wide a compass as I have wandered, I do now gladly overtake and close in with my subject, and shall henceforth hold on with it an even pace to the end of my journey, except some beautiful prospect appears within sight of my way, whereof, though at present I have neither warning nor expectation, yet upon such an accident, come when it will, I shall beg my reader's favour and company, allowing me to conduct him through it along with myself. For in writing it is as in travelling. If a man is in haste to be at home (which I acknowledge to be none of my case, having never so little business as when I am there), if his horse be tired with long riding and ill ways, or be naturally a jade, I advise him clearly to make the straightest and the commonest road, be it ever so dirty; but then surely we must own such a man to be a scurvy companion at best. He spatters himself and his fellow-travellers at every step. All their thoughts, and wishes, and conversation turn entirely upon the subject of their journey's end, and at every splash, and plunge, and stumble they heartily wish one another at the devil.

On the other side, when a traveller and his horse are in heart and plight, when his purse is full and the day before him, he takes the road only where it is clean or convenient, entertains his company there as agreeably as he can, but upon the first occasion carries them along with him to every delightful scene in view, whether of art, of Nature, or of both; and if they chance to refuse out of stupidity or weariness, let them jog on by themselves, and be d—n'd. He'll overtake them at the next town, at which arriving, he rides furiously through, the men, women, and children run out to gaze, a hundred noisy curs run barking after him, of which, if he honours the boldest with a lash of his whip, it is rather out of sport than revenge. But should some sourer mongrel dare too near an approach, he receives a salute on the chaps by an accidental stroke from the courser's heels, nor is any ground lost by the blow, which sends him yelping and limping home.

I now proceed to sum up the singular adventures of my renowned Jack, the state of whose dispositions and fortunes the careful reader does, no doubt, most exactly remember, as I last parted with them in the conclusion of a former section. Therefore, his next care must be from two of the foregoing to extract a scheme of notions that may best fit his understanding for a true relish of what is to ensue.

Jack had not only calculated the first revolution of his brain so prudently as to give rise to that epidemic sect of Æolists, but succeeding also into a new and strange variety of conceptions, the fruitfulness of his imagination led him into certain notions which, although in appearance very unaccountable, were not without their mysteries and their meanings, nor wanted followers to countenance and improve them. I shall therefore be extremely careful and exact in recounting such material passages of this nature as I have been able to collect either from undoubted tradition or indefatigable reading, and shall describe them as graphically as it is possible, and as far as notions of that height and latitude can be brought within the compass of a pen. Nor do I at all question but they will furnish plenty of noble matter for such whose converting imaginations dispose them to reduce all things into types, who can make shadows—no thanks to the sun—and then mould them into substances—no thanks to philosophy—whose peculiar talent lies in fixing tropes and allegories to the letter, and refining what is literal into figure and mystery.

Jack had provided a fair copy of his father's will, engrossed in form upon a large skin of parchment, and resolving to act the part of a most dutiful son, he became the fondest creature of it imaginable. For although, as I have often told the reader, it consisted wholly in certain plain, easy directions about the management and wearing of their coats, with legacies and penalties in case of obedience or neglect, yet he began to entertain a fancy that the matter was deeper and darker, and therefore must needs have a great deal more of mystery at the bottom. "Gentlemen," said he, "I will prove this very skin of parchment to be meat, drink, and cloth, to be the philosopher's stone and the universal medicine." In consequence of which raptures he resolved to make use of it in the most necessary as well as the most paltry occasions of life. He had a way of working it into any shape he pleased, so that it served him for a nightcap when he went to bed, and for an umbrella in rainy weather. He would lap a piece of it about a sore toe; or, when he had fits, burn two inches under his nose; or, if anything lay heavy on his stomach, scrape off and swallow as much of the powder as would lie on a silver penny—they were all infallible remedies. With analogy to these refinements, his common talk and conversation ran wholly in the praise of his Will, and he circumscribed the utmost of his eloquence within that compass, not daring to let slip a syllable without authority from thence. Once at a strange house he was suddenly taken short upon an urgent juncture, whereon it may not be allowed too particularly to dilate, and being not able to call to mind, with that suddenness the occasion required, an authentic phrase for demanding the way to the back, he chose rather, as the more prudent course, to incur the penalty in such cases usually annexed; neither was it possible for the united rhetoric of mankind to prevail with him to make himself clean again, because, having consulted the will upon this emergency, he met with a passage near the bottom (whether foisted in by the transcriber is not known) which seemed to forbid it.

He made it a part of his religion never to say grace to his meat, nor could all the world persuade him, as the common phrase is, to eat his victuals like a Christian.

He bore a strange kind of appetite to snap-dragon and to the livid snuffs of a burning candle, which he would catch and swallow with an agility wonderful to conceive; and by this procedure maintained a perpetual flame in his belly, which issuing in a glowing steam from both his eyes, as well as his nostrils and his mouth, made his head appear in a dark night like the skull of an ass wherein a roguish boy hath conveyed a farthing-candle, to the terror of his Majesty's liege subjects. Therefore he made use of no other expedient to light himself home, but was wont to say that a wise man was his own lanthorn.

He would shut his eyes as he walked along the streets, and if he happened to bounce his head against a post or fall into the kennel (as he seldom missed either to do one or both), he would tell the gibing apprentices who looked on that he submitted with entire resignation, as to a trip or a blow of fate, with whom he found by long experience how vain it was either to wrestle or to cuff, and whoever durst undertake to do either would be sure to come off with a swingeing fall or a bloody nose. "It was ordained," said he, "some few days before the creation, that my nose and this very post should have a rencounter, and therefore Providence thought fit to send us both into the world in the same age, and to make us countrymen and fellow-citizens. Now, had my eyes been open, it is very likely the business might have been a great deal worse, for how many a confounded slip is daily got by man with all his foresight about him. Besides, the eyes of the understanding see best when those of the senses are out of the way, and therefore blind men are observed to tread their steps with much more caution, and conduct, and judgment than those who rely with too much confidence upon the virtue of the visual nerve, which every little accident shakes out of order, and a drop or a film can wholly disconcert; like a lanthorn among a pack of roaring bullies when they scour the streets, exposing its owner and itself to outward kicks and buffets, which both might have escaped if the vanity of appearing would have suffered them to walk in the dark. But further, if we examine the conduct of these boasted lights, it will prove yet a great deal worse than their fortune. It is true I have broke my nose against this post, because Providence either forgot, or did not think it convenient, to twitch me by the elbow and give me notice to avoid it. But let not this encourage either the present age of posterity to trust their noses unto the keeping of their eyes, which may prove the fairest way of losing them for good and all. For, O ye eyes, ye blind guides, miserable guardians are ye of our frail noses; ye, I say, who fasten upon the first precipice in view, and then tow our wretched willing bodies after you to the very brink of destruction. But alas! that brink is rotten, our feet slip, and we tumble down prone into a gulf, without one hospitable shrub in the way to break the fall—a fall to which not any nose of mortal make is equal, except that of the giant Laurcalco, who was Lord of the Silver Bridge. Most properly, therefore, O eyes, and with great justice, may you be compared to those foolish lights which conduct men through dirt and darkness till they fall into a deep pit or a noisome bog."

This I have produced as a scantling of Jack's great eloquence and the force of his reasoning upon such abstruse matters.

He was, besides, a person of great design and improvement in affairs of devotion, having introduced a new deity, who has since met with a vast number of worshippers, by some called Babel, by others Chaos, who had an ancient temple of Gothic structure upon Salisbury plain, famous for its shrine and celebration by pilgrims.

When he had some roguish trick to play, he would down with his knees, up with his eyes, and fall to prayers though in the midst of the kennel. Then it was that those who understood his pranks would be sure to get far enough out of his way; and whenever curiosity attracted strangers to laugh or to listen, he would of a sudden bespatter them with mud.

In winter he went always loose and unbuttoned, and clad as thin as possible to let in the ambient heat, and in summer lapped himself close and thick to keep it out.

In all revolutions of government, he would make his court for the office of hangman-general, and in the exercise of that dignity, wherein he was very dexterous, would make use of no other vizard than a long prayer.

He had a tongue so musculous and subtile, that he could twist it up into his nose and deliver a strange kind of speech from thence. He was also the first in these kingdoms who began to improve the Spanish accomplishment of braying; and having large ears perpetually exposed and erected, he carried his art to such a perfection, that it was a point of great difficulty to distinguish either by the view or the sound between the original and the copy.

He was troubled with a disease the reverse to that called the stinging of the tarantula, and would run dog-mad at the noise of music, especially a pair of bagpipes. But he would cure himself again by taking two or three turns in Westminster Hall, or Billingsgate, or in a boarding-school, or the Royal Exchange, or a state coffee-house.

He was a person that feared no colours, but mortally hated all, and upon that account bore a cruel aversion to painters, insomuch that in his paroxysms as he walked the streets, he would have his pockets loaded with stones to pelt at the signs.

Having from his manner of living frequent occasions to wash himself, he would often leap over head and ears into the water, though it were in the midst of the winter, but was always observed to come out again much dirtier, if possible, than he went in.

He was the first that ever found out the secret of contriving a soporiferous medicine to be conveyed in at the ears. It was a compound of sulphur and balm of Gilead, with a little pilgrim's salve.

He wore a large plaister of artificial caustics on his stomach, with the fervour of which he could set himself a groaning like the famous board upon application of a red-hot iron.

He would stand in the turning of a street, and calling to those who passed by, would cry to one, "Worthy sir, do me the honour of a good slap in the chaps;" to another, "Honest friend, pray favour me with a handsome kick in the rear;" "Madam, shall I entreat a small box in the ear from your ladyship's fair hands?" "Noble captain, lend a reasonable thwack, for the love of God, with that cane of yours over these poor shoulders." And when he had by such earnest solicitations made a shift to procure a basting sufficient to swell up his fancy and his sides, he would return home extremely comforted, and full of terrible accounts of what he had undergone for the public good. "Observe this stroke," said he, showing his bare shoulders; "a plaguy janissary gave it me this very morning at seven o'clock, as, with much ado, I was driving off the Great Turk. Neighbours mine, this broken head deserves a plaister; had poor Jack been tender of his noddle, you would have seen the Pope and the French King long before this time of day among your wives and your warehouses. Dear Christians, the Great Moghul was come as far as Whitechapel, and you may thank these poor sides that he hath not—God bless us—already swallowed up man, woman, and child."

It was highly worth observing the singular effects of that aversion or antipathy which Jack and his brother Peter seemed, even to affectation, to bear towards each other. Peter had lately done some rogueries that forced him to abscond, and he seldom ventured to stir out before night for fear of bailiffs. Their lodgings were at the two most distant parts of the town from each other, and whenever their occasions or humours called them abroad, they would make choice of the oddest, unlikely times, and most uncouth rounds that they could invent, that they might be sure to avoid one another. Yet, after all this, it was their perpetual fortune to meet, the reason of which is easy enough to apprehend, for the frenzy and the spleen of both having the same foundation, we may look upon them as two pair of compasses equally extended, and the fixed foot of each remaining in the same centre, which, though moving contrary ways at first, will be sure to encounter somewhere or other in the circumference. Besides, it was among the great misfortunes of Jack to bear a huge personal resemblance with his brother Peter. Their humour and dispositions were not only the same, but there was a close analogy in their shape, their size, and their mien; insomuch as nothing was more frequent than for a bailiff to seize Jack by the shoulders and cry, "Mr. Peter, you are the king's prisoner;" or, at other times, for one of Peter's nearest friends to accost Jack with open arms: "Dear Peter, I am glad to see thee; pray send me one of your best medicines for the worms." This, we may suppose, was a mortifying return of those pains and proceedings Jack had laboured in so long, and finding how directly opposite all his endeavours had answered to the sole end and intention which he had proposed to himself, how could it avoid having terrible effects upon a head and heart so furnished as his? However, the poor remainders of his coat bore all the punishment. The orient sun never entered upon his diurnal progress without missing a piece of it. He hired a tailor to stitch up the collar so close that it was ready to choke him, and squeezed out his eyes at such a rate as one could see nothing but the white. What little was left of the main substance of the coat he rubbed every day for two hours against a rough-cast wall, in order to grind away the remnants of lace and embroidery, but at the same time went on with so much violence that he proceeded a heathen philosopher. Yet after all he could do of this kind, the success continued still to disappoint his expectation, for as it is the nature of rags to bear a kind of mock resemblance to finery, there being a sort of fluttering appearance in both, which is not to be distinguished at a distance in the dark or by short-sighted eyes, so in those junctures it fared with Jack and his tatters, that they offered to the first view a ridiculous flaunting, which, assisting the resemblance in person and air, thwarted all his projects of separation, and left so near a similitude between them as frequently deceived the very disciples and followers of both. . . *Desunt nonnulla*, . . .

The old Sclavonian proverb said well that it is with men as with asses; whoever would keep them fast must find a very good hold at their ears. Yet I think we may affirm, and it hath been verified by repeated experience, that—

"Effugiet tamen hæc sceleratus vincula Proteus."

It is good, therefore, to read the maxims of our ancestors with great allowances to times and persons; for if we look into primitive records we shall find that no revolutions have been so great or so frequent as those of human ears. In former days there was a curious invention to catch and keep them, which I think we may justly reckon among the *artes perditæ*; and how can it be otherwise, when in these latter centuries the very species is not only diminished to a very lamentable degree, but the poor remainder is also degenerated so far as to mock our skilfullest tenure? For if only the slitting of one ear in a stag hath been found sufficient to propagate the defect through a whole forest, why should we wonder at the greatest consequences, from so many loppings and mutilations to which the ears of our fathers and our own have been of late so much exposed? It is true, indeed, that while this island of ours was under the dominion of grace, many endeavours were made to improve the growth of ears once more among us. The proportion of largeness was not only looked upon as an ornament of the outward man, but as a type of grace in the inward. Besides, it is held by naturalists that if there be a protuberancy of parts in the superior region of the body, as in the ears and nose, there must be a parity also in the inferior; and therefore in that truly pious age the males in every assembly, according as they were gifted, appeared very forward in exposing their ears to view, and the regions about them; because Hippocrates tells us that when the vein behind the ear happens to be cut, a man becomes a eunuch, and the females were nothing backwarder in beholding and edifying by them; whereof those who had already used the means looked about them with great concern, in hopes of conceiving a suitable offspring by such a prospect; others, who stood candidates for benevolence, found there a plentiful choice, and were sure to fix upon such as discovered the largest ears, that the breed might not dwindle between them. Lastly, the devouter sisters, who looked upon all extraordinary dilatations of that member as protrusions of zeal, or spiritual excrescences, were sure to honour every head they sat upon as if they had been cloven tongues, but especially that of the preacher, whose ears were usually of the prime magnitude, which upon that account he was very frequent and exact in exposing with all advantages to the people in his rhetorical paroxysms, turning sometimes to hold forth the one, and sometimes to hold forth the other; from which custom the whole operation of preaching is to this very day among their professors styled by the phrase of holding forth.

Such was the progress of the saints for advancing the size of that member, and it is thought the success would have been every way answerable, if in process of time a cruel king had not arose, who raised a bloody persecution against all ears above a certain standard; upon which some were glad to hide their flourishing sprouts in a black border, others crept wholly under a periwig; some were slit, others cropped, and a great number sliced off to the stumps. But of this more hereafter in my general "History of Ears," which I design very speedily to bestow upon the public.

From this brief survey of the falling state of ears in the last age, and the small care had to advance their ancient growth in the present, it is manifest how little reason we can have to rely upon a hold so short, so weak, and so slippery; and that whoever desires to catch mankind fast must have recourse to some other methods. Now he that will examine human nature with circumspection enough may discover several handles, whereof the six senses afford one apiece, beside a great number that are screwed to the passions, and some few riveted to the intellect. Among these last, curiosity is one, and of all others affords the firmest grasp; curiosity, that spur in the side, that bridle in the mouth, that ring in the nose of a lazy, an impatient, and a grunting reader. By this handle it is that an author should seize upon his readers; which as soon as he hath once compassed, all resistance and struggling are in vain, and they become his prisoners as close as he pleases, till weariness or dulness force him to let go his grip.

And therefore I, the author of this miraculous treatise, having hitherto, beyond expectation, maintained by the aforesaid handle a firm hold upon my gentle readers, it is with great reluctance that I am at length compelled to remit my grasp, leaving them in the perusal of what remains to that natural oscitancy inherent in the tribe. I can only assure thee, courteous reader, for both our comforts, that my concern is altogether equal to thine, for my unhappiness in losing or mislaying among my papers the remaining part of these memoirs, which consisted of accidents, turns, and adventures, both new, agreeable, and surprising, and therefore calculated in all due points to the delicate taste of this our noble age. But alas! with my utmost endeavours I have been able only to retain a few of the heads. Under which there was a full account how Peter got a protection out of the King's Bench, and of a reconcilement between Jack and him, upon a design they had in a certain rainy night to trepan brother Martin into a spunging-house, and there strip him to the skin. How Martin, with much ado, showed them both a fair pair of heels. How a new warrant came out against Peter, upon which Jack left him in the lurch, stole his protection, and made use of it himself. How Jack's tatters came into fashion in court and city; how he got upon a great horse and ate custard. But the particulars of all these, with several others which have now slid out of my memory, are lost beyond all hopes of recovery. For which misfortune, leaving my readers to condole with each other as far as they shall find it to agree with their several constitutions, but conjuring them by all the friendship that has passed between us, from the title-page to this, not to proceed so far as to injure their healths for an accident past remedy, I now go on to the ceremonial part of an accomplished writer, and therefore by a courtly modern least of all others to be omitted.

The Conclusion

Going too long is a cause of abortion as effectual, though not so frequent, as going too short, and holds true especially in the labours of the brain. Well fare the heart of that noble Jesuit who first adventured to confess in print that books must be suited to their several seasons, like dress, and diet, and diversions; and better fare our noble notion for refining upon this among other French modes. I am living fast to see the time when a book that misses its tide shall be neglected as the moon by day, or like mackerel a week after the season. No man has more nicely observed our climate than the bookseller who bought the copy of this work. He knows to a tittle what subjects will best go off in a dry year, and which it is proper to expose foremost when the weather-glass is fallen to much rain. When he had seen this treatise and consulted his almanac upon it, he gave me to understand that he had manifestly considered the two principal things, which were the bulk and the subject, and found it would never take but after a long vacation, and then only in case it should happen to be a hard year for turnips. Upon which I desired to know, considering my urgent necessities, what he thought might be acceptable this month. He looked westward and said, "I doubt we shall have a bit of bad weather. However, if you could prepare some pretty little banter (but not in verse), or a small treatise upon the it would run like wildfire. But if it hold up, I have already hired an author to write something against Dr. Bentley, which I am sure will turn to account."

At length we agreed upon this expedient, that when a customer comes for one of these, and desires in confidence to know the author, he will tell him very privately as a friend, naming whichever of the wits shall happen to be that week in the vogue, and if Durfey's last play should be in course, I had as lieve he may be the person as Congreve. This I mention, because I am wonderfully well acquainted with the present relish of courteous readers, and have often observed, with singular pleasure, that a fly driven from a honey-pot will immediately, with very good appetite, alight and finish his meal on an excrement.

I have one word to say upon the subject of profound writers, who are grown very numerous of late, and I know very well the judicious world is resolved to list me in that number. I conceive, therefore, as to the business of being profound, that it is with writers as with wells. A person with good eyes can see to the bottom of the deepest, provided any water be there; and that often when there is nothing in the world at the bottom besides dryness and dirt, though it be but a yard and half under ground, it shall pass, however, for wondrous deep, upon no wiser a reason than because it is wondrous dark.

I am now trying an experiment very frequent among modern authors, which is to write upon nothing, when the subject is utterly exhausted to let the pen still move on; by some called the ghost of wit, delighting to walk after the death of its body. And to say the truth, there seems to be no part of knowledge in fewer hands than that of discerning when to have done. By the time that an author has written out a book, he and his readers are become old acquaintance, and grow very loathe to part; so that I have sometimes known it to be in writing as in visiting, where the ceremony of taking leave has employed more time than the whole conversation before. The conclusion of a treatise resembles the conclusion of human life, which has sometimes been compared to the end of a feast, where few are satisfied to depart *ut plenus vitæ conviva*. For men will sit down after the fullest meal, though it be only to dose or to sleep out the rest of the day. But in this latter I differ extremely from other writers, and shall be too proud if, by all my labours, I can have any ways contributed to the repose of mankind in times so turbulent and unquiet as these. Neither do I think such an employment so very alien from the office of a wit as some would suppose; for among a very polite nation in Greece there were the same temples built and consecrated to Sleep and the Muses, between which two deities they believed the strictest friendship was established.

I have one concluding favour to request of my reader, that he will not expect to be equally diverted and informed by every line or every page of this discourse, but give some allowance to the author's spleen and short fits or intervals of dulness, as well as his own, and lay it seriously to his conscience whether, if he were walking the streets in dirty weather or a rainy day, he would allow it fair dealing in folks at their ease from a window, to criticise his gate and ridicule his dress at such a juncture.

In my disposure of employments of the brain, I have thought fit to make invention the master, and to give method and reason the office of its lackeys. The cause of this distribution was from observing it my peculiar case to be often under a temptation of being witty upon occasion where I could be neither wise nor sound, nor anything to the matter in hand. And I am too much a servant of the modern way to neglect any such opportunities, whatever pains or improprieties I may be at to introduce them. For I have observed that from a laborious collection of seven hundred and thirty-eight flowers and shining hints of the best modern authors, digested with great reading into my book of common places, I have not been able after five years to draw, hook, or force into common conversation any more than a dozen. Of which dozen the one moiety failed of success by being dropped among unsuitable company, and the other cost me so many strains, and traps, and ambages to introduce, that I at length resolved to give it over. Now this disappointment (to discover a secret), I must own, gave me the first hint of setting up for an author, and I have since found among some particular friends that it is become a very general complaint, and has produced the same effects upon many others. For I have remarked many a towardly word to be wholly neglected or despised in discourse, which hath passed very smoothly with some consideration and esteem after its preferment and sanction in print. But now, since, by the liberty and encouragement of the press, I am grown absolute master of the occasions and opportunities to expose the talents I have acquired, I already discover that the issues of my observanda begin to grow too large for the receipts. Therefore I shall here pause awhile, till I find, by feeling the world's pulse and my own, that it will be of absolute necessity for us both to resume my pen.

(In some early editions of "The Tale of a Tub," Swift added, under the title of "What Follows after Section IX.," the following sketch for a "History of Martin.")

THE HISTORY OF MARTIN

The History of Martin

Giving an account of his departure from Jack, and their setting up for themselves, on which account they were obliged to travel, and meet many disasters; finding no shelter near Peter's habitation, Martin succeeds in the North; Peter thunders against Martin for the loss of the large revenue he used to receive from thence; Harry Huff sent Marlin a challenge in fight, which he received; Peter rewards Harry for the pretended victory, which encouraged Harry to huff Peter also; with many other extraordinary adventures of the said Martin in several places with many considerable persons.

With a digression concerning the nature, usefulness, and necessity of wars and quarrels.

How Jack and Martin, being parted, set up each for himself. How they travelled over hills and dales, met many disasters, suffered much from the good cause, and struggled with difficulties and wants, not having where to lay their head; by all which they afterwards proved themselves to be right father's sons, and Peter to be spurious. Finding no shelter near Peter's habitation, Martin travelled northwards, and finding the Thuringians, a neighbouring people, disposed to change, he set up his stage first among them, where, making it his business to cry down Peter's powders, plasters, salves, and drugs, which he had sold a long time at a dear rate, allowing Martin none of the profit, though he had been often employed in recommending and putting them off, the good people, willing to save their pence, began to hearken to Martin's speeches. How several great lords took the hint, and on the same account declared for Martin; particularly one who, not having had enough of one wife, wanted to marry a second, and knowing Peter used not to grant such licenses but at a swingeing price, he struck up a bargain with Martin, whom he found more tractable, and who assured him he had the same power to allow such things. How most of the other Northern lords, for their own private ends, withdrew themselves and their dependants from Peter's authority, and closed in with Martin. How Peter, enraged at the loss of such large territories, and consequently of so much revenue, thundered against Martin, and sent out the strongest and most terrible of his bulls to devour him; but this having no effect, and Martin defending himself boldly and dexterously, Peter at last put forth proclamations declaring Martin and all his adherents rebels and traitors, ordaining and requiring all his loving subjects to take up arms, and to kill, burn, and destroy all and every one of them, promising large rewards, &c., upon which ensued bloody wars and desolation.

How Harry Huff, lord of Albion, one of the greatest bullies of those days, sent a cartel to Martin to fight him on a stage at Cudgels, quarter-staff, backsword, &c. Hence the origin of that genteel custom of prize-fighting so well known and practised to this day among those polite islanders, though unknown everywhere else. How Martin, being a bold, blustering fellow, accepted the challenge; how they met and fought, to the great diversion of the spectators; and, after giving one another broken heads and many bloody wounds and bruises, how they both drew off victorious, in which their example has been frequently imitated by great clerks and others since that time. How Martin's friends applauded his victory, and how Lord Harry's friends complimented him on the same score, and particularly Lord Peter, who sent him a fine feather for his cap, to be worn by him and his successors as a perpetual mark for his bold defence of Lord Peter's cause. How Harry, flushed with his pretended victory over Martin, began to huff Peter also, and at last downright quarrelled with him about a wench. How some of Lord Harry's tenants, ever fond of changes, began to talk kindly of Martin, for which he mauled them soundly, as he did also those that adhered to Peter. How he turned some out of house and hold, others he hanged or burnt, &c.

How Harry Huff, after a deal of blustering, wenching, and bullying, died, and was succeeded by a good-natured boy, who, giving way to the general bent of his tenants, allowed Martin's notions to spread everywhere, and take deep root in Ambition. How, after his death, the farm fell into the hands of a lady, who was violently in love with Lord Peter. How she purged the whole country with fire and sword, resolved not to leave the name or remembrance of Martin. How Peter triumphed, and set up shops again for selling his own powders, plasters, and salves, which were now declared the only true ones, Martin's being all declared counterfeit. How great numbers of Martin's friends left the country, and, travelling up and down in foreign parts, grew acquainted with many of Jack's followers, and took a liking to many of their notions and ways, which they afterwards brought back into ambition, now under another landlady, more moderate and more cunning than the former.

How she endeavoured to keep friendship both with Peter and Martin, and trimmed for some time between the two, not without countenancing and assisting at the same time many of Jack's followers; but finding, no possibility of reconciling all the three brothers, because each would be master, and allow no other salves, powders, or plasters to be used but his own, she discarded all three, and set up a shop for those of her own farm, well furnished with powders, plasters, salves, and all other drugs necessary, all right and true, composed according to receipts made by physicians and apothecaries of her own creating, which they extracted out of Peter's, and Martin's, and Jack's receipt-books, and of this medley or hodge-podge made up a dispensatory of their own, strictly forbidding any other to be used, and particularly Peter's, from which the greatest part of this new dispensatory was stolen. How the lady, farther to confirm this change, wisely imitating her father, degraded Peter from the rank he pretended as eldest brother, and set up herself in his place as head of the family, and ever after wore her father's old cap with the fine feather he had got from Peter for standing his friend, which has likewise been worn with no small ostentation to this day by all her successors, though declared enemies to Peter. How Lady Bess and her physicians, being told of many defects and imperfections in their new medley dispensatory, resolve on a further alteration, to purge it from a great deal of Peter's trash that still remained in it, but were prevented by her death. How she was succeeded by a North-Country farmer, who pretended great skill in the managing of farms, though he could never govern his own poor little farm, nor yet this large new one after he got it. How this new landlord, to show his valour and dexterity, fought against enchanters, weeds, giants, and windmills, and claimed great honour for his victories. How his successor, no wiser than he, occasioned great disorders by the new methods he took to manage his farms. How he attempted to establish in his Northern farm the same dispensatory used in the Southern, but miscarried, because Jack's powders, pills, salves, and plasters were there in great vogue.

How the author finds himself embarrassed for having introduced into his history a new sect different from the three he had undertaken to treat of; and how his inviolable respect to the sacred number three obliges him to reduce these four, as he intends to do all other things, to that number; and for that end to drop the former Martin and to substitute in his place Lady Bess's institution, which is to pass under the name of Martin in the sequel of this true history. This weighty point being cleared, the author goes on and describes mighty quarrels and squabbles between Jack and Martin; how sometimes the one had the better and sometimes the other, to the great desolation of both farms, till at last both sides concur to hang up the landlord, who pretended to die a martyr for Martin, though he had been true to neither side, and was suspected by many to have a great affection for Peter.

A Digression on the Nature, Usefulness, and Necessity of Wars and Quarrels

This being a matter of great consequence, the author intends to treat it methodically and at large in a treatise apart, and here to give only some hints of what his large treatise contains. The state of war, natural to all creatures. War is an attempt to take by violence from others a part of what they have and we want. Every man, fully sensible of his own merit, and finding it not duly regarded by others, has a natural right to take from them all that he thinks due to himself; and every creature, finding its own wants more than those of others, has the same right to take everything its nature requires. Brutes, much more modest in their pretensions this way than men, and mean men more than great ones. The higher one raises his pretensions this way, the more bustle he makes about them, and the more success he has, the greater hero. Thus greater souls, in proportion to their superior merit, claim a greater right to take everything from meaner folks. This the true foundation of grandeur and heroism, and of the distinction of degrees among men. War, therefore, necessary to establish subordination, and to found cities, kingdoms, &c., as also to purge bodies politic of gross humours. Wise princes find it necessary to have wars abroad to keep peace at home. War, famine, and pestilence, the usual cures for corruption in bodies politic. A comparison of these three—the author is to write a panegyric on each of them. The greatest part of mankind loves war more than peace. They are but few and mean-spirited that live in peace with all men. The modest and meek of all kinds always a prey to those of more noble or stronger appetites. The inclination to war universal; those that cannot or dare not make war in person employ others to do it for them. This maintains bullies, bravoes, cut-throats, lawyers, soldiers, &c. Most professions would be useless if all were peaceable. Hence brutes want neither smiths nor lawyers, magistrates nor joiners, soldiers or surgeons. Brutes having but narrow appetites, are incapable of carrying on or perpetuating war against their own species, or of being led out in troops and multitudes to destroy one another. These prerogatives proper to man alone. The excellency of human nature demonstrated by the vast train of appetites, passions, wants, &c., that attend it. This matter to be more fully treated in the author's panegyric on mankind.

The History of Martin—*Continued*

How Jack, having got rid of the old landlord, set up another to his mind, quarrelled with Martin, and turned him out of doors. How he pillaged all his shops, and abolished his whole dispensatory. How the new landlord laid about him, mauled Peter, worried Martin, and made the whole neighbourhood tremble. How Jack's friends fell out among themselves, split into a thousand parties, turned all things topsy-turvy, till everybody grew weary of them; and at last, the blustering landlord dying, Jack was kicked out of doors, a new landlord brought in, and Martin re-established. How this new landlord let Martin do what he pleased, and Martin agreed to everything his pious landlord desired, provided Jack might be kept low. Of several efforts Jack made to raise up his head, but all in vain; till at last the landlord died, and was succeeded by one who was a great friend to Peter, who, to humble Martin, gave Jack some liberty. How Martin grew enraged at this, called in a foreigner and turned out the landlord; in which Jack concurred with Martin, because this landlord was entirely devoted to Peter, into whose arms he threw himself, and left his country. How the new landlord secured Martin in the full possession of his former rights, but would not allow him to destroy Jack, who had always been his friend. How Jack got up his head in the North, and put himself in possession of a whole canton, to the great discontent of Martin, who finding also that some of Jack's friends were allowed to live and get their bread in the south parts of the country, grew highly discontented with the new landlord he had called in to his assistance. How this landlord kept Martin in order, upon which he fell into a raging fever, and swore he would hang himself or join in with Peter, unless Jack's children were all turned out to starve. Of several attempts to cure Martin, and make peace between him and Jack, that they might unite against Peter; but all made ineffectual by the great address of a number of Peter's friends, that herded among Martin's, and appeared the most zealous for his interest. How Martin, getting abroad in this mad fit, looked so like Peter in his air and dress, and talked so like him, that many of the neighbours could not distinguish the one from the other; especially when Martin went up and down strutting in Peter's armour, which he had borrowed to fight Jack. What remedies were used to cure Martin's distemper. . .

Here the author being seized with a fit of dulness, to which he is very subject, after having read a poetical epistle addressed to. . . it entirely composed his senses, so that he has not writ a line since.

N.B.—Some things that follow after this are not in the MS., but seem to have been written since, to fill up the place of what was not thought convenient then to print.

A Project for the Universal Benefit of Mankind

The author, having laboured so long and done so much to serve and instruct the public, without any advantage to himself, has at last thought of a project which will tend to the great benefit of all mankind, and produce a handsome revenue to the author. He intends to print by subscription, in ninety-six large volumes in folio, an exact description of *Terra Australis incognita*, collected with great care, and prints from 999 learned and pious authors of undoubted veracity. The whole work, illustrated with maps and cuts agreeable to the subject, and done by the best masters, will cost but one guinea each volume to subscribers, one guinea to be paid in advance, and afterwards a guinea on receiving each volume, except the last. This work will be of great use for all men, and necessary for all families, because it contains exact accounts of all the provinces, colonies, and mansions of that spacious country, where, by a general doom, all transgressors of the law are to be transported; and every one having this work may choose out the fittest and best place for himself, there being enough for all, so as every one shall be fully satisfied.

The author supposes that one copy of this work will be bought at the public charge, or out of the parish rates, for every parish church in the three kingdoms, and in all the dominions thereunto belonging. And that every family that can command £10 per annum, even though retrenched from less necessary expenses, will subscribe for one. He does not think of giving out above nine volumes nearly; and considering the number requisite, he intends to print at least 100,000 for the first edition. He is to print proposals against next term, with a specimen, and a curious map of the capital city with its twelve gates, from a known author, who took an exact survey of it in a dream. Considering the great care and pains of the author, and the usefulness of the work, he hopes every one will be ready, for their own good as well as his, to contribute cheerfully to it, and not grudge him the profit he may have by it, especially if he comes to a third or fourth edition, as he expects it will very soon.

He doubts not but it will be translated into foreign languages by most nations of Europe, as well as Asia and Africa, being of as great use to all those nations as to his own; for this reason he designs to procure patents and privileges for securing the whole benefit to himself from all those different princes and states, and hopes to see many millions of this great work printed in those different countries and languages before his death.

After this business is pretty well established, he has promised to put a friend on another project almost as good as this, by establishing insurance offices everywhere for securing people from shipwreck and several other accidents in their voyage to this country; and these officers shall furnish, at a certain rate, pilots well versed in the route, and that know all the rocks, shelves, quicksands, &c., that such pilgrims and travellers may be exposed to. Of these he knows a great number ready instructed in most countries; but the whole scheme of this matter he is to draw up at large and communicate to his friend.

A NOTE ABOUT THE AUTHOR

Jonathan Swift (1667–1745) was an Irish poet and satirical writer. When the spread of Catholicism in Ireland became prevalent, Swift moved to England, where he lived and worked as a writer. Due to the controversial nature of his work, Swift often wrote under pseudonyms. In addition to his poetry and satirical prose, Swift also wrote for political pamphlets and since many of his works provided political commentary this was a fitting career stop for Swift. When he returned to Ireland, he was ordained as a priest in the Anglican church. Despite this, his writings stirred controversy about religion and prevented him from advancing in the clergy.

A NOTE FROM THE PUBLISHER

Spanning many genres, from non-fiction essays to literature classics to children's books and lyric poetry, Mint Edition books showcase the master works of our time in a modern new package. The text is freshly typeset, is clean and easy to read, and features a new note about the author in each volume. Many books also include exclusive new introductory material. Every book boasts a striking new cover, which makes it as appropriate for collecting as it is for gift giving. Mint Edition books are only printed when a reader orders them, so natural resources are not wasted. We're proud that our books are never manufactured in excess and exist only in the exact quantity they need to be read and enjoyed.

Discover more of your favorite classics with Bookfinity™.

- Track your reading with custom book lists.
- Get great book recommendations for your personalized Reader Type.
- Add reviews for your favorite books.
- AND MUCH MORE!

Visit **bookfinity.com** and take the fun Reader Type quiz to get started.

Enjoy our classic and modern companion pairings!

Printed in the USA
CPSIA information can be obtained
at www.ICGtesting.com
JSHW080001150824
68134JS00021B/2220

9 781513 270272